Economies of
the Heart

ALSO BY CHRISTOPHER ZENOWICH

The Cost of Living

Economies of ···the Heart···

stories

Christopher Zenowich

1817

HARPER & ROW, PUBLISHERS, New York
Grand Rapids, Philadelphia, St. Louis, San Francisco
London, Singapore, Sydney, Tokyo, Toronto

The author wishes to acknowledge the Cornelia Carhart Ward Fellowship of the English Department at Syracuse University for the freedom to write these stories.

"Earning Power" appeared originally in the *Dickinson Review;* "On the Roof" appeared originally in *Graywolf Annual #4.*

FIRST EDITION

Designed by Cassandra J. Pappas

Library of Congress Cataloging-in-Publication Data

Zenowich, Christopher.
　　Economies of the heart / Christopher Zenowich. — 1st ed.
　　　　p.　cm.
　　ISBN 0-06-016243-0
　　I. Title.
PS3576.E537E28　1990
813'.54—dc20　　　　89-45734

90 91 92 93 94 CC/HC 10 9 8 7 6 5 4 3 2 1

For Toby

··*Contents*··

Economies of
the Heart

·· *Think Big* ··

Bob Bodewicz didn't want to be a Boy Scout. They were too groupie. But he loved their magazine, *Boys' Life,* and he asked his Boy Scout friends for their copies after they had finished with them.

He stacked these in a corner of the living room, and returned to them for tips on tying exotic knots and building shelters out of snow, for stories of wilderness survival and heroism during disaster, and for profiles of star athletes. Eventually his mother would insist that he clip and save the articles he wanted and throw away the rest.

It was during one of these purges that Bob noticed a small ad in the back pages of one issue:

MAKE MONEY IN YOUR SPARE TIME

Make extra spending money in your free time by raising chinchillas. It's easy, fun, and guaranteed. Write for free information using the coupon below, and indicate how much extra income you desire. No obligation!

The possibility of freeing himself from allowances and their awful chores appealed to Bob. He didn't know what chinchillas were, but he filled in the coupon, pausing only to consider how much extra income he could use. There were three choices: "Between $1,000 and $2,000," "Between $4,000 and $6,000," and "Over $10,000." He checked the first option and left the coupon on the table for his father to mail the next day.

His father woke him with a shake early on Saturday morning.

"You want me to mail this," he said, holding out the coupon. His forehead was wrinkled and his voice was gruff.

Bob couldn't think of anything he'd done wrong, so he nodded.

"Where's the envelope?"

"Could you do it?"

His father looked at the coupon; then at Bob. "If you want me to fill out the envelope, I get to see what you want to mail, and I don't approve."

Bob couldn't imagine his father not approving. Money was money.

"What is this, anyway?" his father continued. "You want to make just a thousand? You can't live on a thousand. What do you think this is? The eighteen hundreds? For chrissake, if you're going to think at all, think big. That's what separates the winners from the losers in this world. As long as you've got winners and losers, you've got competition. Free enterprise. If there's no risk, there's no gain. So think big." He took a pen from his pocket and crossed out Bob's choice, and checked the box for "Over $10,000." Then he

stared briefly at what he had done. "There, you see, that's
the spirit."

Bob got up and watched his father leave. His father was
big. Fat Frank, his friends called him.

A few weeks later on one of the first warm spring days,
Bob's mother announced that a man had called.

"He said he'd received our coupon, and that he wanted
to pay us a visit to discuss our interest in chinchillas," she
said, giving her head a shake to knock her one gray bang
to the side.

"I thought they were going to send information first,"
his father said. "What did you say?"

"I asked him when he wanted to drop by, and he said
he'd be in the area just a couple more days and how about
tomorrow night."

"Tomorrow? Not tomorrow, it's Friday, for chrissake. I
bowl." His father mopped his plate clean with a piece of
bread and then looked at Bob. "You finished with that?"
He pointed to the remains of a pork chop on Bob's plate.
Bob said nothing. His father took it and began gnawing at
the bone, stripping off the last fibers of meat, his lips
shiny.

"Who's coming?" Carl asked.

Bob glared at him. He was so stupid. Why hadn't he been
listening?

"No one's coming," his father said. "Not tomorrow."
When Bob's father made up his mind, that was usually the
end of discussion.

"I'm afraid he's coming whether you go bowling or not,"
his mother said, holding three dirty plates on her way to

the kitchen. His father handed her the pork chop bone, chewed clean.

"Call him back and cancel," he said, and then belched: "Bow-wow."

"Can't," his mother said from the kitchen. "No number." It wasn't like her to be so matter-of-fact in contradicting his father.

"Who doesn't have a number?" Carl asked.

"Ellie, you're not meeting with him without me here. I don't want you getting suckered into some deal by a slick talker."

"Who's coming?" Carl asked.

"Just go look at your bird books," Bob said.

He never saw the hand coming. It snapped his head back, stinging his cheek and sending white spots into his eyes.

"Watch your lip," his father said. "It was your idea, you know. And Carl could help you with it."

"Who's coming?" Carl asked, this time softer.

"The chinchilla guy, dammit," his father said. "Don't you listen?"

Carl kept his head down, and traced a wrinkle in the blue plastic tablecloth. Bob was close to not caring anymore. Getting smacked just for saying that, it wasn't fair. "So you're not going bowling?" his mother said, wiping her hands on her apron. She stared at Bob. He was fighting back tears. She turned to his father. "You'll be here?"

"What choice do I have? First, mister mail order sends off for information. And then you invite a stranger into our house. What choice do I have?"

"He said he rarely has someone as interested as we are.

4

He asked if we live on a farm. What did you put on that coupon, anyway, Bob?"

Carl and his mother both stared at him. Bob felt like everyone was blaming him. He looked at his father, who was ignoring everyone. He didn't dare say anything about how the coupon had been changed. His father wiped his mouth and belched the words, "Scussi mwah."

The chinchilla man was due at seven, right after Walter Cronkite. Everyone sat in the living room, waiting. Carl was gluing together a model of a rose-breasted grosbeak. Bob's mother looked at a magazine in her chair. His father wrinkled his forehead and reread the sports page. Bob sat there, standing every few minutes when a car went down the road. The new electric coffeepot gurgled in the kitchen. There were small white donuts on a plate, too.

After twenty minutes, Bob's father began snapping the pages of the newspaper as he turned them. Finally, he tossed the paper on the floor.

"Please, Frank, I just picked up," his mother said.

"And I canceled my bowling night," he said, folding his arms across his chest. He did this whenever he was ready to argue.

Carl saw the car first. "Wow," he said. Everyone went to the door.

It was big. It barely fit on their dirt driveway.

"What is it?" Bob asked.

"One of those brand-new Caddys," his father said. "The guy must be rakin' it in."

The car was a well-polished powder blue, with shiny chrome, twin headlights, a fancy hood ornament and large fins with huge taillights shaped like flying saucers. It had New Jersey plates. Bob had never been to New Jersey, but for a brief moment, his spirits lifted at the prospect of making thousands of dollars in his spare time, it seemed to him like a land of great opportunity.

"He must be Italian," Bob's mother said, watching from the front door as the man got out of the driver's seat and waved to her.

"What's the matter," his father said. "He too successful for your tastes?"

Bob opened the door and stood on the steps, watching the man. He was big, too. He wore a blue suit just a bit darker than his Cadillac, and the tail of his white shirt dangled below his jacket at his back.

"Son," the man said, opening the trunk. "How about lending me a hand here?" The man smiled at Bob and waved him over. Seal, Bob's Lab, woofed from the steps.

"C'mere, lady," the man said to the dog. "How about one of these?" He handed her a biscuit.

The trunk was dark and deep like a cave, and packed with neatly organized boxes. Bob was certain this would be better than selling Christmas cards.

"Ivan Helgren," the man said, extending his hand. "And you are . . .?"

"Bob," he said. The man squeezed his hand until it hurt. "The one who wrote."

"Oh," the man said. "You wrote, huh? You got an older brother?"

"Nope, I'm the oldest."

"That a fact," he said. He lifted a green case and a rolled-up movie screen out of the trunk. "I take it your dad's a farmer out here?"

"Naw, he works in a factory," Bob said, taking a heavy black case that the man handed to him.

Mr. Helgren looked at him for a second, then up at the front door where Bob's mother and father stood. He shook his head quickly and said, "Well, sport, let's get going. I'm heading out of state tonight, back home."

Mr. Helgren introduced himself to everyone else and accepted a cup of black coffee to which he added four teaspoons of sugar. He drank it straight down, then stood up and stretched himself.

"That certainly hits the spot," he said. "Now, where should I set up the movie?"

"Gee, I don't know," Bob's mother said. "We've never had a movie in the house before. Let me clear an area." She pushed the TV to one side of the living room and dragged the coffee table to the rear. It was warm and humid and Bob saw a trickle of sweat making its way down her forehead. She was exhaling deeply, and Bob wondered if she were trying to get his father's attention.

"You two get in there and help your mother," Bob's father said to Carl and him. They put down their half-finished second donuts and went into the living room.

"Good boys," Mr. Helgren said. "They look like the kind that would like to raise chinchillas."

Bob watched as Mr. Helgren looked out the rear window into the back field. He was helping his brother drag a chair across the living room into the dining room, and the slip-cover started to pull off.

"Please, boys, let me do this," his mother said, picking up dust balls and two small plastic soldiers from where the chair had been. Bob and Carl returned to the dining room and took their seats at the table.

"I don't see a barn back here," Mr. Helgren said. "Maybe you could point me in the right direction."

"Not unless you've got a good imagination," Bob's father said. "We don't have one."

"But you were interested in making more than ten grand a year, if I recall," Mr. Helgren said.

"That's correct."

"Hmmm. How about your cellar? Maybe we could fit them in your cellar."

"If it means making ten grand a year, we could put 'em in our bedrooms," Bob's father said. He laughed at his own joke. Bob saw his mother stand up straight and smooth out her dress. She was listening intently now.

"Do you mind if I take a look at the basement?" Mr. Helgren asked.

"Not at all," Bob's father said.

"It's such a mess, though," Bob's mother said. "We're ready to see the movie."

"We'll be right back up," Mr. Helgren said. "I just want to size out your cellar. Bob, you've seen a movie screen set up in school, haven't you?"

Bob nodded.

"Good boy. Why don't you try to set up this one."

While Bob's father and Mr. Helgren were down in the

cellar, Bob's mother helped him stand the screen and open it up.

"I'm getting madder by the minute," she was saying. "Your father needs to talk to me about this."

Carl was sliding a torn hassock from the bedroom down the hallway. Bob could hear fragments of the discussion in the cellar. He could make out a "considering" and "profit."

"Don't you bring that in here," Bob's mother said to Carl. "I want that out of sight. And, be quiet. Carry it, don't slide it." She was standing perfectly still between the living room and dining room, staring now into space and listening. Carl ignored her.

"Take that back to the bedroom," Bob whispered at Carl. "Both of you, shhhh!"

The men were climbing the stairs. As they came up through the kitchen, Mr. Helgren was speaking and his father was nodding.

"As I was saying," he went on, "ten grand a year might be a little steep for the space you've got. But two hundred cages, about one per cinder block along the north wall, why that ought to generate close to six grand a year. I can get into the numbers and contractual arrangements in a few minutes after the movie. Before I show it, might I use your bathroom?"

Bob's father pointed him to the door and took a seat in the living room, right next to Carl on the couch. Bob's mother went over to him.

"What are you doing?" she whispered. "We don't even know what's involved with these things. Why are you acting like we're going to do this?" She went to the hutch and pulled out her silver horn-tipped glasses, which she wore only when a life insurance salesman was visiting.

"What's your problem," he said.

"Shhhh," she hissed as Mr. Helgren emerged from the bathroom, the toilet in the final throes of a flush. "Maybe we should take a seat at the table while we discuss this," she announced.

"We got a movie here, don't we, Ivan?" Bob's father said. "Let's watch the movie."

"That's right, Frank," Mr. Helgren said. "If you don't mind, ma'am, I thought we'd watch the movie first. That way, you'll have an accurate idea about what's involved with running a money-making chinchilla operation in a home like yours." He set up the projector and started the movie. It was called *The Chinchilla Story: There's Gold in Those There Furs.*

"Since the days of the earliest Spanish settlers in Chile and Peru," the movie began, "since the rise of the grand Incan empires, the chinchilla has been valued for its soft, pearly gray fur. . . ."

A small creature about the size of a squirrel was shown sipping water from a metal pan and nibbling on food.

"It looks like a rat," Bob's mother said.

Mr. Helgren chuckled. "Nothing like a rat, ma'am," he said. "Clean and friendly these things are."

The movie showed how thousands of Americans today made extra money by raising chinchillas in their spare time. "Today, Americans know, as did the ancient Incas, 'there's gold in those there furs,' " the movie concluded. The film clicked through the projector, and the screen went white.

In the glare of the screen Bob's mother appeared expressionless. She had her arms folded, and she was tapping her foot.

"What do you think?" Bob's father said to him, rubbing his head. "You want to try it?"

Bob looked at his mother, who pushed her glasses up the bridge of her nose and stared at him. He couldn't bring himself to speak. Not when he could see his mother was angry. First his father, now his mother. And all he wanted was a way to make money. How could things be going so wrong?

"Don't need to answer just yet, son," Mr. Helgren said. "Let me tell you a little more about them." He packed up the screen and the projector, leaving them by the front door, and then brought a briefcase over to the dining room table.

"Ellie, how about a little of that coffee," Bob's father said.

"That sounds good to me," Mr. Helgren said, opening the briefcase and pulling out some papers. He looked them over in silence, waiting for Bob's mother to return with a tray holding the coffeepot and cups. She dropped the tray on the table with a thwack, and Bob's father looked up at her in surprise. Mr. Helgren didn't seem to notice.

"First, I'd like to know, Bob," Mr. Helgren said, "what do you think? You still interested in making thousands of dollars a year raising chinchillas?"

Bob nodded. That was the whole point of the night. But he felt like there was something else going on, just beyond his knowing.

"You certain about that, Bob?" Mr. Helgren asked. "You don't seem too certain."

"I'm certain," Bob said.

"Of course you are," Mr. Helgren said. "In fact . . ."

"Just a second," Bob's mother said. "Let's talk over some of the details. How do we raise these things? Let 'em run around downstairs and throw the food to them? And what kind of time will it take? These boys want to go to college. They don't want to spend their evenings feeding these things when they should be studying."

"I was just getting to that, ma'am," Mr. Helgren said.

"C'mon, Ellie, give him a chance, will you?" Bob's father said. "It's for the kids."

For the first time that night, Bob felt like his father was on his side. It was for him. And for Carl, too. It would be their money, he hoped. In the bank for them.

"First, though, I'd like you to feel this," Mr. Helgren said, lifting a compartment in his briefcase and pulling out a gray fur. "Go ahead, feel it."

Everyone took turns feeling it. Carl took two turns.

"You ever feel anything so soft?" Mr. Helgren said.

"No," Carl said, rubbing it on his cheek.

Mr. Helgren reached inside his jacket and pulled out another gray fur. "And that's not even a chinchilla fur," he said. "Feel that against a real chinchilla fur."

"Wow," Carl said.

Everyone took turns feeling the real chinchilla fur.

"Huh," Bob's father said, the last to feel. "That's really something."

"You can say that again, Frank," Mr. Helgren said. "I know you can see why these chinchilla furs are so valuable. And why there's money to be made raising them."

"Make a nice pair of underwear," Bob's father said.

Mr. Helgren laughed. "Never thought of that, Frank. Maybe we should put you on the marketing council. But we do know they make a nice coat. Wouldn't you agree, Ellie?"

She didn't answer his question. There was a moment of silence. "Just how do we raise them?" she asked, pushing up her glasses.

"I was getting to that," Mr. Helgren said. "As you can see here"—he slid a piece of paper with a chart on it across the table—"you've got space for two hundred cages, and with one total turnover per year, that gives you four hundred pelts worth a minimum wholesale of ten-fifty per pelt. . . ."

Bob's father whistled.

"That's right, Frank, we're talking in the vicinity of forty-two hundred a year, gross. Now, don't stake me to this, but in my opinion, with the mink disease they're having out West, we could see these pelts going up another two bucks per in the next year."

Bob tried to imagine what he could do with that much money.

He would be the most popular kid in the school. He'd be able to buy a car of his own when he was sixteen. He'd be able to buy presents whenever he wanted.

"Where do the cages come from?" Bob's mother asked as she inspected the chart.

"We supply 'em," Mr. Helgren said, pulling out several other sheets of paper. "Along with the food, the medicine, and all the technical support you need. You got a question, call us collect, twenty-four hours a day."

"That's sounds like a helluva support system to me,"

ECONOMIES OF THE HEART

Bob's father said. He shifted in his chair.

"I'm glad you brought that up," Mr. Helgren said, "because that's what we're here for. As a support group for our growers. A resource for your every need."

"How do we pay for all this?" Bob's mother asked.

"As you can see from this," Mr. Helgren said, sliding another chart across the table, "there are several ways, the simplest being a fourteen-thousand-dollar up-front investment on your part for the cages and a four-year feed contract that calls for a specially developed, nutritionally balanced chinchilla feed not available anywhere else in this country."

"It seems like an awful lot of money," Bob's mother said.

"You've got to spend money to make money," Bob's father snapped. "Christ, I can see that at the plant."

"I'm glad you mentioned that, Frank," Mr. Helgren said. "You're right, too, Ellie, if I may. That's why we've developed a special four-year payment plan that enables you to keep ten percent of your gross revenue until the cages and feed contracts are all paid off. At that point, the profits are all yours, minus, of course, the feed, medicine, and litters that we keep you supplied with."

"And how much does that run?" she asked.

"Approximately fifteen hundred a year," Mr. Helgren said, taking out another chart with blanks and the heading "Profit Potential." He took a blue magic marker and deducted the number fifteen hundred from forty-eight hundred. He looked up at Bob's father and slid the chart slowly toward him. "That leaves you with a minimum of thirty-three hundred, free and clear. Your labor . . ." He looked at Bob and Carl. "Why, that's free and clear, too, isn't it?

You boys are ready to make money, aren't you?"

Bob and Carl nodded. Bob picked up the chinchilla fur and felt it against the other gray fur. Ten-fifty per pelt. Just a small fur, no bigger than a squirrel's. His head was swimming with numbers. It was better than the frontier days. He knew his mother didn't like the idea, but she could get used to it. She'd gotten used to other things before, like the dog. She hadn't wanted Seal at first. But Bob promised to take care of it, and he had. He'd manage with the chinchillas. And, he'd keep up with his schoolwork, too. She'd see.

"How much work are these animals?" Bob's mother asked. Eyeing Frank, she added, "How clean are they?"

"That's a good question, and one I'm frequently asked by the lady of the house," Mr. Helgren said. "The truth is, if you keep their water and their cages clean every other day, they're cleaner than hamsters. And I'd be happy to supply you with the phone numbers of a few growers who do raise them in their cellars just like you will. Why, I've seen some shipments of pelts arrive that I felt didn't even need to be washed, although we clean each batch as a matter of principle."

"Who does the skinning?" Bob's mother asked.

"We supply you with a special skinning apparatus the size of a toaster," Mr. Helgren said. "Takes it off quicker than you can pull the skin off a chicken."

"And the bodies? What about the bodies?"

"Simply dispose of them, ma'am," Mr. Helgren said, shifting in his chair.

"Oh, no," she said. She shook her head quickly. "Hundreds of bloody chinchillas stuffed in the garbage cans. The stink would be unbearable."

"The stink wouldn't be that bad," Bob's father said, shaking his hand as if he were refusing a cup of coffee. "Not for that kind of money."

"We can do it, Mom," Bob said. "Right, Carl?"

This time, Carl said nothing. He looked at Bob, then at his mother, then back at Bob.

"I think we need some time to think about this," Bob's mother said. "Among ourselves."

"Of course," Mr. Helgren said. "It's a major decision you're talking about. I should tell you, though, that we are going to keep our membership restricted to maintain the quality and price of our pelts. Based on your interest, we've reserved a membership for you. However, we can honor this reservation only for a limited time. I think you understand. Now I'd be happy to wait in my car for a half hour or so if you'd like to discuss this, but I'm afraid that I'm going to have to ask that you answer us tonight."

"In that case, the answer is no," Bob's mother said.

"Oh no it isn't," Bob's father said. "We'll talk about it."

Bob's hopes fell and rose with each speaker. Things were too touchy to dare adding a word. He had seen his mother bring things to a halt before. Once she put her mind to it, she could overcome the momentum of almost anything.

"Who exactly is the 'we' you keep referring to," Bob's mother said to Mr. Helgren. She sounded suddenly calmer. That worried Bob more than her earlier uneasiness.

"I haven't told you? Why, please excuse my oversight." He pulled out a certificate from his briefcase. "I'm with the Chinchilla Growers Guild of America. The CGGA, more than thirteen hundred members, and, since nineteen fifty-seven, the voice of the chinchilla grower in Washington."

"I'd say we're very interested in reaching an agreement tonight," Bob's father said.

"Did you say 'guild'?" Bob's mother asked, calmer still and pushing up her glasses.

"Yes, I did," Mr. Helgren said. "Have you heard of us, the Chinchilla Growers Guild of America?"

"Not specifically of you," Bob's mother said. "But I have heard a thing or two about guilds."

"They're a marvelous concept in money-making for everyone involved," Mr. Helgren said.

"I don't know," Bob's mother said. "The whole thing sounds kind of foreign to me. The Incas, Chile, Peru, and now a guild. Let me think. . . ." She took off her glasses and stared at the ceiling. "Yes, I'm quite sure now, guild has something to do with the communists."

"What?" Mr. Helgren said. "Nothing could be . . ."

"Carl," Bob's mother said. "Go look up 'guild' in the dictionary and tell me what you find."

Carl ran into the living room.

"There's nothing even remotely communist about this organization, ma'am," Mr. Helgren said. "Why, we're dedicated to making money. You understand, don't you, Frank?"

"Sure, I guess," Bob's father said. But he turned his eyes away from Mr. Helgren and stared down at the tablecloth. *Communism* was a powerful word in the house, something which instantly turned friendly conversations serious. "She knows a lot about them. The communists, that is. She's read Ayn Rand."

Carl returned holding the dictionary open. "It says an association of people bound by a common goal or shared interests, as in medieval guilds," he reported.

"See," Bob's mother said. "A common goal, shared interests, the whole thing goes against the individual."

Mr. Helgren brought his hand down on the table. "I don't know where you get your ideas, lady, but this is the last thing we're out to do."

"Look up China, Carl," Bob's mother said. "See if it says anything about guilds. Then check Russia."

Mr. Helgren was sweeping up his papers. "Lady, you don't have the slightest idea what you're talking about."

Bob's father stood up, knocking his chair over backward. "You're a guest in this house, mister, but that doesn't give you the right to talk to my wife like that. I suggest you leave."

"You won't have to ask me twice," Mr. Helgren said. "I've never been received like this before."

"China has guilds, too," Carl said, bringing in the encyclopedia.

Mr. Helgren began yanking up his papers and charts, stuffing them into his briefcase. "I can't believe I've wasted a call on rednecks like you."

"Now just a second," Bob's father said, poking his finger in Mr. Helgren's chest. "Where do you get off talking like that? I'm beginning to think my wife's right about you. What kind of name is that, anyway, 'Ivan'?"

"You want to know what kind of name that is? It goes with Patulsky, not Helgren. It's Polish."

"I knew it all the time," Bob's father said. "You can't hide it."

"People trust Scandinavians in the fur business, that's

all," Mr. Helgren said. "Nothing more than that. I'm from Paterson. Christ, John Wayne is a made-up name."

"I've heard enough out of you," Bob's father said.

"You think it's a treat for me?" Mr. Helgren asked. "Just let me out of here."

Bob and Carl got out of the way as their father quickly followed Mr. Helgren—the movie screen tucked under one arm, one hand holding the projector, the other his brief-case. He banged his way out the door. He opened the back door of the Cadillac and tossed everything across the seat. Bob's father stood on the front steps, his arms folded, as if supervising the exit to make sure everything proceeded according to orders. The engine of the Cadillac revved, its lights came on. Then it retreated quickly, kicking up dust and stones as it spun out of the driveway, its tires squealing when they hit the pavement. It paused there on the road, the idle of the engine gradually slowing until the hum of an electric window could be heard. Mr. Helgren's head appeared, a silhouette outlined by the glow of the dashboard lights.

"Never again will you have a chance with us," he shouted. "You're nothing. Not even prospects." The window hummed back up, the transmission popped into drive, and the Cadillac swooshed down the road, its ruby red brake lights casting a pink glow over the fins. Bob watched the lights, wanting them to somehow be clues to a new life, one away from the lawns he mowed and the rewinding tape of talk about bad supervisors and dumb bosses. How he wished there was a way to make money without giving in to all that.

Bob's mother was picking up the coffee cups when Mr. Helgren spoke his final words. She snorted as if clearing her sinuses.

"Tough darts to you, too," she said.

"I think you were onto something, Mom," Carl said. "You got under his skin."

"You think so, sweetie?" She hugged Carl and winked at Bob, and took the cups to the kitchen. Bob's father had retaken his seat on the couch, newspaper again in hand. His mother returned and pushed the TV back to its place, a neat square of dust on the floor at the center of the far wall.

"I'm glad that's behind us," she said.

"How did you know, Mom?" Carl asked.

"Oh, I guess I did what I had to."

"That's right," Bob's father said, setting down the paper. "And to think he drove a Caddy, too. Talk about a wolf in sheep's clothing."

"Exactly," she said. She hummed the first four notes of Beethoven's Fifth as she straightened out the living room.

"Let it be a lesson to you boys," Bob's father said. "Be prepared."

"Prepared!" Carl shouted.

"Drop!" Bob's father said.

And as if they had choreographed it, Bob and Carl hit the floor and began their push-ups. One after another, down and up, down and up. Carl weakened first. Bob could see his arms wobbling, his rear arching upward, his face contorted almost clownishly in agony.

"One more," Frank said with a military snap to his voice, and Carl sank again and barely rose, this time only to collapse in exhaustion.

Bob continued. Ten more. And another five. Until he too felt his arms burning, the heels of his hands aching, his sight dimming.

"One more," his father said again.

Bob sank and tried. He tried harder.

"C'mon, one more."

"Honestly, Frank," his mother said. "He's trying."

"Trying doesn't count."

Bob dipped. He felt his rear moving up, but nothing else.

"C'mon, defeatist, a Russian boy could do one more. You can't be weak."

No, Bob couldn't be weak. He closed his eyes, strained until he saw spots, and in his imagination, rose one last time.

·· *Pete the Painter* ··

*A*ll I'm saying is, don't discourage the boy," Uncle George repeated, taking a napkin from his lap to dab at the edge of his mouth.

"So you think that all this mess"—Bob's mother paused to point to the rocks that he had toted home from riverbeds and gravel banks—"could lead to something worthwhile?"

George raised his fork as if to say, Who can tell? "You know who you should talk to is old . . ." George paused to watch Bob's father, who waved his hand to interrupt while he swallowed a mouthful of mashed potatoes.

"But the point is," Bob's father said finally, "if he's going to lug all these rocks back to the house, he's got to keep them in some kind of order. Not strewn over the living room and on the front step. I almost broke my neck tripping over them."

"So give him a place in the cellar to keep them," George said. "A shelf. But give him the knowledge to sort them out, too."

Bob hated it when adults discussed his future without consulting with him. He looked over at Carl, who dropped his jaw slowly and then snapped it shut like a lizard catching a fly. He opened it again as he forked in some mashed potatoes, letting them sit on his tongue.

"Eat right or go to bed," Bob's mother said.

Carl snapped his jaw shut and grinned. Bob shut his eyes to avoid his brother's stare.

Frank asked Carl to pass him the bread. "I read somewhere that there's more gold in the silt of the Sacramento River than in Fort Knox," he said, putting a slice of bread on his plate and spearing it with his fork. He mopped up juice from the steak. "Trouble is, you can't get it out for what it's worth." With one swift motion, he put the soggy bread into his mouth and swallowed it.

"Exactly," Uncle George said. "Not yet, anyway. But someone will come along with a practical way to get it done sooner or later. And there's lots of places like that, too. The old nickel mine, for instance."

"What old nickel mine?" Bob asked.

"The one over on Prospect Mountain," he said. "Off Cathole Road."

Bob looked over at his father. "You never told me there was a mine up there."

"It's just a hole in the ground. Flooded."

"Until someone comes up with a way to get the water out," George said. "And maybe there's another mineral up there that no one knows about. They found uranium in a lot of those old gold mines. But it was never worth anything until the bomb."

"Maybe one of those rocks has uranium in it," Carl said.

"Well, now," George said, "there's no way for us to tell until one of us understands geology better, is there?"

"Are there any books we can get him?" Bob's mother asked.

George explored a charred piece of steak with his knife and, finding nothing salvageable there, set his utensils on the plate. "He might be better off with a tutor. Isn't old Pete a geologist by training?"

"Pete the Painter?" Frank asked. "A geologist?"

"Yeah," George said. "With the Army Corps of Engineers. He surveyed the mineral formations found when they built the Alaskan Highway. He told me once that there's enough gold in the mountains up there to make a man rich—if he has the nerve to live alone in the wilderness for two years."

"You think he could tutor Bob, Ellie?" Frank asked. His forehead wrinkled at the thought of it.

Bob's mother turned to George, her voice dropping to her candid tone: "We hear he's a terrible substitute teacher. The kids ridicule him."

"Let's face it, the guy's a flake," Frank said. "Eccentric. Maybe even nuts. If he knows where that gold is, what the hell is he doing living around here?"

"When you're talking about any of those old families it's tough to say who's nuts and who's not," Ellie said. "He's very sick—severe arthritis. He's been in the hospital with it."

"There you go," George said immediately. "Bob's ready to give him a chance."

"It's not his chance to give," Frank said. "He won't be writing the checks to Pete, I will. And if Pete tutors like he paints, we won't get squat for the deal."

George dabbed his mouth with a napkin, raising his eyebrows. "It's your choice," he said. "The boy's expressed a natural interest in stones. Geologists make a good living, you know. Looking for gold, for oil, you name it. Heck, Old Colonel Randolph—it was his old man who dug that mine on Prospect Mountain—he told me there was enough nickel ore up there to make a man rich. What I'm really suggesting is that you've got a chance here to put a little knowledge together for a reasonable investment with the potential for big payoff. I've always believed that if you want the big score, you've got to find a shortcut. These guys with their shoulders to the wheel every day, what the hell do they get out of life? You've got to leapfrog the mundane if you want to find the spectacular."

Everyone stopped eating. Even the dog beneath the table seemed to have stopped panting. Carl's mouth was closed. Bob wondered whether everyone thought, as he did, that George's speech was aimed right at his father. Ellie began tapping her fingers.

"Is that a fact?" Bob's father said finally.

"I think so," George said. "I've never believed you got anything for hard work except hard luck. Our backs are weak and our knees gimpy. But we've got brains and we should use them more than we do to turn our fortunes around. And this mine is just one instance. If it's loaded with nickel like Randolph claimed, let Bob learn how to get it out."

"So why not send somebody up there with pumps and drain the thing?" Frank said. "We could probably get the land for a song."

"You're missing the point," Bob's mother said. "Really. This mine isn't the point. Education, any education at all can never be bad. The more you learn, the more opportunities there are."

"Precisely," George said. "The mine's an example, that's all. An example of what somebody who knew geology could be doing. There are probably a dozen spots in northwestern Connecticut that a geologist would be smart to spend some time at. But I don't know them—and neither do you. We've got to know more, and Bob's willing, aren't you?"

"My only concern is that he might be too sick to take on Bob," Ellie continued. "When the arthritis flares up, it can be pretty bad."

"So we'll send him there with some aspirin," Frank said. "What's the big deal?"

Pete the Painter wasn't a painter and his name wasn't Pete. A substitute teacher no one respected, he fancied himself as an inventor. His great patent was a plow that popped up when the blade hit a rock. A big farm tractor company bought it from him. That had been years ago. Lately the inventions hadn't been going too well. People in town said that he had more than twenty patents, but all for things no one would dream of manufacturing: rotating storage shelves for kitchen cabinets, a gauge for an automobile dashboard that displayed tire air pressure as a function of temperature. He owed his nickname to one of his inventions—a paint that would never peel. When he painted a neighbor's barn for free as a demonstration it subsequently peeled in a year. If he hadn't done it for free, no one would have tolerated him. As it was, he was the best dreamer in Litchfield, a town of dull dreams and old money.

Pete lived alone in a large granite farmhouse his great-great-great-grandfather constructed in 1817. His family had lived there ever since, generation after generation. All of them were farmers until Pete. Besides Pete, there was a sister in New Haven who worked for the Salvation Army. No one had seen her in years.

In addition to his infamous paint, Pete was also known by the men around town for one other feat: Every Fourth of July, the story went, Pete dropped by the American Legion Hall for the picnic, which was by tradition short on food and long on beer. Late, after the women had packed up and gone home, leaving their husbands to humor one another with their fibs and fancies and poker games, Pete, his New England instinct for reserved behavior long flushed away, would ask for a moment of silence before exclaiming, "Gentlemen, to our flag," and then turn to a bystander and ask that the pinky finger on his right hand be tugged. As Pete faced the flag and his finger was tugged, he'd fart the first five notes of "The Star-Spangled Banner."

"You could tune a piano by it," Bob's Little League coach told his father, who'd never been present for the concert.

• • •

On the last Saturday of June, Bob walked to Pete's house. He took a check made out to Wilbur Warner for nine dollars to cover three hours of tutoring scheduled to begin at 9:30. But Bob got started late and didn't get there until 10:00. He didn't know which door to knock on. There was one in front, and two on the side, all of which appeared equally used. The sounds of sloshing water led Bob to the back of the house.

Bob found Pete lowering a wood post into a pit filled with an acrid, bright orange liquid. He wore an old green workshirt rolled at the sleeves and dirty painter's overalls.

"Bob, you're here already," he said, not looking at his watch. "You can help me. Grab that other post back there." He pointed to the side of a shed where a row of wood posts stripped of bark stood propped against the wall. Bob dragged one over to Pete, who harnessed it with a chain tress and lowered it into the pit. He wasn't as big or as barrel chested as Bob remembered. His hair, cut short as a Marine's, had receded and turned completely gray, although it didn't look bad against his well-tanned skin.

"What is this stuff?" Bob asked.

"My latest experiment," he said, rising and turning his head in a complete circle. "Oh, this body of mine."

"What's that stuff do to the posts?"

"Treats them. Makes them oblivious to the assault of the elements." He twisted his neck from side to side, and opened and closed his hands. "If only it were safe to drink, huh? The elixir we've all been looking for."

"But what is the stuff? Why is it orange?"

"Ahh, there wouldn't be much point to a new invention if everyone knew what was in it, now, would there?"

Bob shook his head, wondering what any of this had to do with geology. "Here," he said, handing Pete the check.

Pete held the check before his face as if it were written in a foreign language. "Well, what is it you're here for?"

"Geology?"

"Don't you know?" Pete's face twitched in pain. His arm jerked up suddenly and the check slipped from his fingers. Bob lunged and caught it just before it zigzagged into the pit.

"Oh, you're like a bird," Pete said. "I would gladly give you what I know of rocks to move like that again."

Bob fell silent, ignorant of how to summon the words of sympathy appropriate for a grown man's pain. Pete's eyebrows twitched upward, governed by their own logic, in no relation to the expression on the rest of his face. He looked oddly transformed from the daydreamer who'd substituted for Bob's regular fifth grade teacher more than a year ago. That man swung his legs up on the desk and talked and talked while the class troublemakers roamed idly in the back, shooting spitballs and singing "Oh, say can you see" to the flatulent percussion of hands squeezed in armpits. Pete remained silent during it all until Billy O'Connor, a plumber's son, yanked Becky Saunders's pigtail. In what seemed like a second, Pete spun across the desk and, traversing the classroom in barnyard strides, grabbed Billy with one hand and lifted him off his feet.

This Pete was thinner, the wrinkles in his face were more snarled, his steps more cautious, as if the earth might give way at any second.

• • •

"Yes, geology, then," he said quietly, almost muttering. "Your mother's a sweetheart. Known her since she was a girl. Her father, your grandfather, helped me once. Built a nifty little wooden prototype of an irrigator pump I'd tried to sell. No one bought it. But the prototype was a piece of art. I still have it." He glanced at the roof of his house. "Up there, I guess. I don't know. Haven't been in the attic in years." He paused and said something to himself. "Okay, then, geology."

Pete wandered over to the house, kicking along the high weeds that grew by the round stone foundation. He stooped, balancing himself against the side of the house, and picked up a dirty bell jar. He dipped it into the pit, holding up a cup of orange liquid before Bob's face. "What do you say—a mixture or suspension?"

"I don't know."

"You know the difference, don't you?"

Bob shook his head.

"You know some chemistry at least, don't you? The periodic table? The parts of an atom?"

Bob had heard of these things, and knew something about the atom, but he didn't want to be quizzed. So he shook his head again.

Pete led Bob into the house. The place was cool and messy, the air stale with the scent of mildew and wet newspapers. There were file folders, buckets, tools, old feed bags, and oddly shaped pieces of metal scattered throughout the room. It took a minute for Bob to realize he was in a kitchen. He couldn't find the stove, but assumed it was somewhere beneath a pile. Dirty plates and glasses were stacked in the sink, and on the counter next to it, a random formation of empty Campbell's Pork 'N Beans cans, some on their sides, some standing, all with their lids popped open and erect. Wherever Bob stepped, spumes of dust erupted into the air, illuminated by the shafts of sunlight that slanted in through the large windows over the sink.

Pete rummaged through the piles, searching for something. "Here it is," he said at last. "Chemistry for the layman, an intro text. Take it home and read the first chapter for next week. That's your assignment. We'll do one a week. Now for my filing system. A real breakthrough, and simple, too. It's . . ." Pete jerked his head back and sucked in a short breath, his lips twitching. When he got control of himself, he cleared his throat and looked at Bob as if he were seeing him for the first time. It made Bob feel uncomfortable. Then he looked around the kitchen, slowly lifting papers and putting them back carefully, as if their chaotic appearance were a premeditated pattern.

"If I asked you to file something in this," he said, picking up a small green file card holder similar to the one Bob's mother used for recipes, "you'd do it alphabetically, right? The lesson we're all taught to do. But it's slow, clumsy. So I came up with my own. I assigned a number to each letter, one through twenty-six, *A* being one, *Z* being twenty-six. It's much faster. And here's a message for you."

Pete took a pencil from his pocket and wrote on an old newspaper: 12-5-19-19-15-14, 15-22-5-18. "Dashes between letters, commas between words. You decipher it."

After a minute of figuring it out, Bob turned to Pete and asked, "That's it for today?"

"Very good," he said. "Isn't it clever? Pretty soon those numbers will mean more than letters to you. Faster. Cleaner. More precise."

Bob nodded, eager to agree, although he couldn't possibly imagine why numbers made for quicker cataloging systems than letters.

The chemistry text was slow reading. The musty smell of its glossy pages made him sleepy and dull. Its black-and-white photos, often stained, showed the same student, a teenaged boy identified as "Richard" in the captions below, his hair slicked back, his pencil-thin black tie unchanged from one photo to the next as he demonstrated good lab procedures and performed experiment after experiment.

"Richard properly angles the test tube of distillate for heating over a Bunsen burner." Or, "Richard oxidizes iron filings and sulfur." And, "Richard cleans test tubes to ready them for a new day of experiments." He tried to imagine what Richard would look like today. Maybe he was Pete.

Bob scrubbed his hands with Comet every time he finished his lesson, trying to remove the book's smell. But it lingered, unfortunately much longer than his memory of the periodic table, valences, isotopes, and flame tests. If this was leapfrogging the mundane, he wanted no part of it.

To make matters worse, Carl let it be known among his friends that Bob took lessons in geology. It wasn't long before the kids teased him nonstop. Being known as a rock hound in seventh grade wasn't exactly the ticket for attracting girls. One Friday afternoon, Billy Carmen, the town

bully, said he had a couple of rocks in his pants he wanted
Bob to take a look at.

Bob got in a fight. It was a typical junior-high thing. A
lot of wild swings, pushing and heavy breathing, each of
them waiting for a teacher to break it up. As Bob was
escorted to the principal's office, it seemed in retrospect
like the fights in women's Roller Derby he had watched
each Saturday on WPIX until he started geology lessons.
Billy and Bob sat on the bench in the principal's office, the
secretaries eyeing them. "Billy, you're no surprise—but
Bob, what are you doing here?"

"Looking for rocks," Carmen said.

The secretary laughed. Bob wanted to hit him, but almost cried instead.

Bob hesitated at the stone wall in front of the house, finally
sitting down on it. He hadn't been there that long before
he heard Pete directly behind him. "You coming up here,
or what," he said.

Bob jumped to attention. "I'm tired," he said.

"What is this? Second thoughts about lessons?"

"Oh, no," Bob said, trying to sound sincere.

Pete shook his head slowly. "Don't fib to me, Bob. I can
hear it. You know, no one who does anything worthwhile
in this world is a popular guy at first. What? The kids find
out you were seeing me? They ask you about 'Pete the
Painter'?"

Bob stared into Pete's face. His eyebrows twitched.
There was no way he could lie.

"I thought so. Probably consider you odd to study rocks. Right?"

Bob told him what had happened.

Pete laughed. "This Carmen boy," he said. "The world is filled with jerks like that. Most of them become politicians and claim it's a nation's pride they're talking about. They come and go. One generation after another. Leaves that fall and rot. But the earth, it swallows them all. Know that and you know everything."

Bob followed Pete toward the house.

That summer between other chores, Pete developed a new tacking compound to seal the eroding mortar between the great granite blocks of his house. Whatever he did, Pete turned it into a lecture about chemistry and geology, especially once it became apparent that Bob wasn't going to master chemistry beyond the most rudimentary level. When he worked with metal, Pete explained the differences between iron and steel, and the ways in which steel refining differed from aluminum refining. When he worked on the pump, he discussed the effect of water in shaping the environment and how seas had once existed where now his house stood. When he retacked the granite blocks of his house, he talked about the compositions of various cementing materials and why they produced concrete when mixed with sand and water.

Gradually the landscape itself became the book they studied. Every outcropping of rock, every bog or river valley, every hill and cliff became a text that Pete read to

Bob, re-creating the colossal tensions and pressures of the
earth's surface and its imperceptible transformations. Everything that had once appeared to Bob as immutable and
everlasting was in fact changing, but in movements so slow
and by forces so titanic that only a trained eye could detect
them. It was as if the earth itself were an organism, containing within it all of the chemicals and forces found in the
human body, which Bob learned from one of the books
Pete lent him had a mineral value of only $1.07.

By the end of the summer, it had become increasingly
difficult to overlook Pete's physical problems. The fingers
of his left hand had curled up because of the arthritis, but
none of the doctors he went to could explain his twitches
and spasms. Bob began taking care of various chores for
Pete during their Saturday sessions. All of his tinkering
came to an end.

"Sounds like Parkinson's to me," Bob's mother said over
dinner one day.

"Oh, crap," Bob's father said. "A goddamn summer of
lessons and he hasn't taken you up to the nickel mine yet?"

"That's not the way he teaches," Bob said. "You never
know what he'll talk about. It depends on what's going on
that day. When I cleaned out his gutters last week, he talked
about how organic material turns into oil, and how to rec-
ognize various land formations as possibilities for drilling.
Every time I ask him when we'll visit the mine, he says,
'Let's take each day as we find it.' "

"That's fine and good for Pete," Frank said. "But I didn't
inherit a farm and a few hundred grand when my old man
died. I can't afford to take each day as I find it."

"He can't, either," Ellie said.

"Baloney," Frank replied.

"It's not baloney. I asked Judy at the bank. She's not supposed to give out that kind of information, but she said he has practically no money. Never has. He's got a big house and a lot of acres."

"Now what made you ask her that?" Frank asked. "You thought the same thing, didn't you?"

Bob's mother fumbled with her fork. "Well . . . I did think it. He hasn't yet cashed a check we've given him."

"What's he use to buy his beans then?" Frank asked. "Listen, don't shed any tears for Pete. He's probably got a mattress somewhere in that house stuffed with ten-dollar bills."

"Wow," Carl said. "Have you seen it?"

Bob smirked at his brother. "Of course not."

Frank cleared his throat and hook shot his napkin into the wastebasket. "My suggestion to you is that you get him up to that mine before he's too sick to move."

That Saturday, while his friends gathered at the schoolyard to play touch football with girls, Bob asked Pete about the nickel mine.

Pete was tired and in too much pain to consider a trip to Prospect Mountain. He had a bottle of aspirin next to him, and every so often, he took a tablet out and chewed it. "That stupid old mine," he said. "People have been asking me about that for years. The only thing you'll find up there are snakes sunning themselves on the rock heaps."

"My uncle George claims Colonel Randolph said there was a good vein of nickel flooded out," Bob said.

Pete shook his head slowly, his eyebrows twitching. "First of all, there is no such thing as a 'vein of nickel.' Only nickel ore. And that nickel ore is poor. Strictly low grade. Do you think for a second somebody wouldn't have drained those shafts if the ore was worth it? Do you?"

Bob shrugged his shoulders. "I guess so."

"Of course so. They've got ore out west in Canada that's twice as rich and half as expensive to process. That's the bottom line with mining, you know. It's a business, Bob. Not a fantasy. If there was ore up there worth the price of mining it, the corporations would be here in a minute, buying off every politician and blowing up that whole mountain until you could put a parking lot in its place. That's the way they mine these days."

"I'd at least like to take a look at it."

"Of course you would. Look at it. Snoop around the scrap heaps. You can find some nice samples of the ore. And while you're there, hike on up past the mine to the top of the mountain. Tell me what you see."

"What do you mean? What am I looking for?"

"Tell me what you find, that's all. I'll find out what you've learned."

Pete balanced himself with his left hand, its fingers frozen inward, as if they were a claw. "I think I've got to try some whiskey or something to cut this pain," he said. "Could you fetch some for me? Beneath the sink?"

Bob opened the cupboard doors beneath the sink. There was a bottle of bourbon next to the dish soap. He took a dirty glass from the sink, washed it out, and poured it half full, the room filling with the dark smell of bourbon. Pete was still shaking.

"I can't hold the glass," he said. "Can you let me drink from it?" Beneath his twitching eyebrows, Pete stared straight into Bob's eyes.

Bob put the glass to Pete's mouth, his lips smacking by themselves now. He slowly tilted the glass until the bourbon moistened Pete's lips and spilled into his mouth. Pete jerked his head back when his mouth was full, swallowing it in one gulp. "The provinces of my body are in revolt," he said.

That week after school Bob hiked up Prospect Mountain. He took a knapsack with him. He was halfway up a slope of loose stone before he realized he was on the scrap heap of the mine. When he got to the top, he looked around, trying to find the entrance. The area was overgrown with brush. The sun had sunk below the crest of the mountain, leaving him in shadow. As he got closer to the face of a forty-foot slab of granite, he suddenly found himself at the edge of a square hole in the ground. Its sides were reinforced with timber. It was a shaft, filled with water, about six feet below.

Bob moved around the shaft, looking for the second one. He found it at the base of the granite slab. Barbed wire, gone limp to rust over the years, surrounded the entrance. This opening, too, was filled with water of an opaque metallic green color, utterly still. Nothing moved across its surface. Not insects, not frogs. He couldn't see beneath the surface for more than an inch. The water looked as poisonous as water could get.

Something about the shafts unsettled Bob. He imagined

them as incredibly deep, and filled with this dark, corrosive water that had filtered through the porous ore within and that now was as ruined as the waste water from an industrial process.

Bob picked up a few samples of ore from the scrap heap and was about to head back down the mountain when he remembered Pete's advice about going all the way to the top. He took a deep breath and headed up. There was something like a path to follow—a notch between two steep faces of rock. He could make out the ripples of ore in the rock, sensing for the first time what the original discoverers of the ore must have felt. One small plateau led to another rise, and, at last, to the summit of Prospect Mountain, a great bald stretch of rock covered in spots with moss. He looked out over hill after hill stretching in purple ripples all the way to Massachusetts.

Bob was certain that Pete had something more in mind than the view. He circled the bald area of rock, about the size of a football field. It was granite like all the rest of the mountain; there was no ore. When he got to the westernmost side of the rock, he turned his back to the sun and saw what Pete had wanted him to see. Etched into the top of Prospect Mountain were several great lines that ran the entire length of the bald spot. Only one thing could have caused them: the glacier. It wasn't that the lines in themselves were interesting. It was that the lines gave him some sense of how large the glaciers were. Here, on the top of this mountain, overlooking the Berkshire foothills all the way north, a sheet of ice had passed. A sheet so large and so heavy it gouged the granite with a signature that all the wind and rain and ice of a hundred thousand years couldn't erase.

Pete got too sick to continue with lessons. Irma, his sister, came up from New Haven to care for him. She called Bob to tell him that Wilbur wanted him to have some fossils she'd found in the basement.

In early October, while Bob's father waited in the car, its exhaust fumes billowing out the rear, Bob knocked on the front door. A tall woman with gray hair wrapped in a bun answered.

"You're Bob?" she asked curtly.

Bob nodded.

"These are yours, then," she said, motioning to two cardboard boxes filled with rocks. Bob stooped and looked at them more closely. Each rock had a fossil in it. Odd snails and crustaceans, the imprint of a leaf, the foot track of a small, four-toed dinosaur. There were more.

"He wants you to take these books, too," she said. It was the chemistry book and several of the geology texts he'd had Bob read.

"Can I thank him?" Bob asked.

There was a sound from upstairs. A creepy sound. It took Bob a second to realize it was Pete's voice. Irma shook her head.

"I have to go now," she said, shutting the door as soon as Bob shifted the boxes and books to the front step.

The leafless limbs of the maple trees clacked overhead in the wind. On the way back to the car, Bob paused and looked around. He could see a light on in the kitchen. Irma had moved in, and folks thought she wasn't too friendly. Bob didn't have anything to say to her anyway.

The gray of the granite blocks merged with that of the sky above. Bob could see the oak behind the house. He remembered walking there with Pete, who leaned against the tree as he pointed to the path the great glacier had cut down through the hillsides that surrounded his farm. Bob's father honked the horn for him to get going. It was getting colder, the wind picking up, time to head back.

As he returned to the car, Bob kept his mind off the wind by thinking of the great rivers of ice that had plowed across the landscape. He tried to imagine the immensity of the silent collisions between drifting continents. To imagine forces beyond his mind's ability to know them, forces that exceeded measurement on the small scales of the most sensitive instruments. He thought of a fire so hot it turned limestone into waxy marble, of a weight so great that it pressed a lump of black carbon into a diamond. Of the infinity it took to render uranium into lead. And as his eyes teared against the wind, he shut them and saw now the great salt seas that had been everywhere and vanished, leaving the oddest codes of all buried in the soft mud of their shores: the faint image of a leaf, an alphabet of bones, the spark that radiated that fiber and flesh lost beneath the shadow of a passing cloud, or in the sudden rupture of the earth's thin tissue.

··*Earning Power*··

*T*he factory was a rambling brick fortress overlooking the river. There was a rocket-shaped water tower on its roof and a rusting Quonset hut in back. From the hut's rear door, carts loaded with broken porcelain fixtures and acid-soaked corncob grounds were dumped. Sometimes on Sundays, when no one was working at the plant, Bob played there while his father filled the soda machines on each of the four floors. That was his extra job. Sometimes Bob helped out by combing the production floor for bottles that had been left behind by the workers. But on this Sunday, Bob was going there to do a job.

He had asked his father for a toy pistol at Al Ducci's Five and Dime. His father refused. He said it was high time Bob started earning his own money for toys. There were plenty of chores to be done at the factory while he was busy with the soda machines. He said he'd pay Bob $1.50 for sweeping around the saws and milling machines on the fourth floor, and then down the entire stairwell to the basement.

"You can earn the rest for the squirt gun by helping your mother around the house this week after school. Is it a deal?"

"What if it's not there?"

"Then you've got two dollars to call your own."

"Dad . . ."

"Don't worry about it. Al will save it. I'll call him from the plant."

Bob wasn't so sure the pistol would be left. Especially if Bernie Wilbur saw it. His father let him get anything he wanted right when he saw it. But Bob's father called Al Ducci from the shipping room and put Bob on the phone.

"I'll set that squirt gun aside for you as soon as I hang up," Mr. Ducci said.

"The Neutralizer, right?" Bob said, worried that Mr. Ducci would set aside one that didn't glow in the dark.

"The Neutralizer," Mr. Ducci said. "And if you can come up with only one-fifty, don't worry about it. I'll let you have it anyway. You can owe me the difference."

Bob had been to the fourth floor only once before. If it were up to him, he'd spend nearly all his time in the plant up on the fourth floor. There were alleyways of stacked boxes and chests filled with old copper and brass electrical parts. The space was used for storage and the occasional sawing or milling of parts for special orders. A layer of brown dust covered everything: boxes, old workbenches, the floor. Even the high tin ceiling was a uniform brown, as if it had been sprayed. And around the saws and milling machines there were piles of dust, dirt, and corkscrewed metal shavings.

"Nobody cleans up after himself up here," his father said. "This is disgusting. Let me find a broom and a dustpan and you can get going."

While his father searched for a broom, Bob wandered over to the windows and looked down on the river below. There was no higher place from which to look at it. The plant was set on the edge of a steep bank leading down to the river, and the sight of the drop was hypnotic. He wanted to open a window and spit, and watch it fall all the way, but he was afraid his father would get angry. Instead, he banged a box next to the window and watched a plume of dust rise.

"Come over here," his father said. "Stop clowning around." His father still could not find a broom.

"Take a look in the infirmary," he said, motioning toward the far wall of the storage area. "See if there's a broom."

The infirmary had two beds. One was empty except for a folded army blanket and a pillow without a cover. The other was loaded with dusty boxes. On top of one was a crossbow. Bob had never seen one in real life. It too was covered with dust. He blew some off and tried to pull back the drawstring, but he couldn't budge it. He carried the bow out to show to his father.

"What are you doing with that," his father said. "Put it back." He was holding a broom in his hand.

"Why is there a crossbow in there?" Bob asked.

"Somebody used to use it on squirrels in back. It doesn't work anymore. It's useless."

"Can I have it?"

"It doesn't belong to us. And it doesn't work. It's just junk. What do you want it for if it doesn't work?"

"To play with."

"Get to work and earn the money you need to buy that toy then. Forget the crossbow."

Bob put the crossbow back and followed his father to the saws and milling machines.

"You got to be careful with this broom," he said, pushing it. Its head came off and tumbled along the floor. "See what I mean? That end won't stay on. I don't know why they do everything so half-assed around here." He put his foot on the broom end and pushed the pole into it. "You put it in like this. You understand?"

Bob nodded.

"Good. I'm going downstairs to start on the soda machines. Sweep up these piles and dump the dirt into the barrels by the window. Then do the stairwell down to the third floor and find me. I want to inspect your work."

When his father left, Bob tried sweeping the sawdust piles together. But they were too big and went right over the top of the broom. When he tried sweeping parts of the piles, things seemed to get worse. The handle kept coming off and kicking up the brown dirt. The air got dustier. He could feel his eyes and nose stinging. He decided to use the dustpan as a shovel. This worked better. But when he dumped the sawdust into the barrels, entire clouds of dirt, round as the barrel tops, puffed up like smoke from a cannon. Pretty soon he couldn't even breathe through his nose. And when he wiped it, he saw that his snot was a dark brown like the colored sawdust.

At last the big piles had been cleaned up and dumped in the barrels. Bob was ready to start on the stairwell. Before he did, though, he went into the infirmary to look at the crossbow once more. He couldn't imagine how anyone could leave something so neat just sitting around in a factory. Were there any arrows for it? He started looking around. There was a metal suitcase on top of the boxes on the bed. He couldn't reach it from the floor, so he climbed on the bed and then onto the boxes to reach it. Suddenly his foot fell into one of the boxes, and he tumbled down, suitcase in hand, his nose banging against the metal frame of the bed. Breathing in deep to avoid crying, he tasted something sour and salty. Tears? Dirt? He didn't know which. The air was full of dust and he was worried that his father had heard. He slid the suitcase under the bed and ran out to the storage area, wiping his eyes on the backs of his sleeves and listening for sounds of his father coming upstairs. There was only the rhythmical hum of a machine from somewhere far below.

Bob went back in and opened the suitcase. Inside were eight metal arrows for the crossbow. Each had soft black feathers. The tips were like V-shaped razor blades. He could kill anything with this—squirrels, cats, dogs that chased him—anything. He wondered whether anyone would miss the crossbow if he took it. He thought for a second about throwing it out the window, but he was afraid it would break open, or slide into the river and float away. He'd have to think of some other way to get it out.

"How you doing up there?" his father yelled from below. "I don't hear anything."

Bob quickly shut the suitcase and slid it under the bed

again, then tiptoed out into the storage area.

"Okay," he said. "I'm ready to start on the stairwell."

"It's about time," his father said, coming up the stairs. "You're going to have to move faster if you want to make money."

Bob stood on the broom, holding its handle straight up and rocking back and forth.

"Don't do that," his father said. "You'll wreck it and then you'll have to pay for it. Let me see what you've done." He walked over to the saws and milling machines and looked around. "It's better than it was, but that's all. It's not clean. You'll have to do a better job on the stairwell. And what have you been doing to yourself? You're a mess. You whack yourself with that handle? I told you to watch out."

He took Bob by the hand and marched him to the men's bathroom at the top of the stairwell. There were two sinks in the bathroom, one of which was filled with pieces of shredded newspaper, string, and sawdust. The green metal waste basket was overflowing with paper towels.

"What is that?" Bob asked, pointing to the sink.

"A rat nest," his father said, rubbing down his face with a wet paper towel.

"Rats?"

"You've seen 'em by the river. Where do you think they live at night?" He held a dry paper towel to Bob's nose. "Blow." Bob blew and his father inspected the towel. Blood was now mixed with the brown snot. "Watch out with that broom. Maybe you're too young to sweep."

"No, I'm okay." He sucked in through his nose, but it was still too clogged to breathe.

His father opened the stall door. "Jesus," he said, flushing the toilet. "What a bunch of slobs in this place." He stood over the toilet with one hand propped against the wall of the stall, peeing. When he reached to zip up his trousers, he squatted slightly, rising as he zipped up. This was different than the way Bob did it. When his father noticed him watching, he waved him off. "Shake a leg now. We've got to get moving. I'm going down to do the machines on the second floor."

Bob watched his father head down the stairs. He began pushing the dirt down to the landing midway between the third and fourth floors. But with each push the broom head slipped down a step, catching on the stair's lip and falling off. After a few steps, he got mad. Only the thought of earning enough money for The Neutralizer kept him going. He decided to sweep backward, walking down the steps and pulling the dirt toward him. This worked much better. By the time he reached the third-floor landing, he had a huge pile of dirt and sawdust, old candy wrappers, and flattened cigarette butts.

His throat was dry now, and he decided to get a drink from the fountain near the third-floor assembly area. This was where the women worked. His father said they had nimble little fingers good for wrapping wires around connectors but that they were hard to supervise. Bob thought about his mother's fingers. They were smaller than his father's, but not as nimble as his.

To get to the fountain, he walked past a caged-in area of old dark brown wooden boxes filled with screws of all sizes and colors. There were golden brass screws and silver-plated steel screws, copper-colored screws and gray rivets, flat heads and round heads. He played there whenever his father let him, pretending the screws were the coins of a secret treasure house. All of it was his. It made his hands slippery with oil and bitter to taste.

The fountain on the third floor was next to a stack of fuse box inner assemblies, waiting to be inserted in the gray metal boxes. The water in this fountain always tasted funny, and there was rust and a green-colored streak in the enamel basin. But Bob was thirsty, and the film in his mouth and throat made the water impossible to taste anyway. He drank long, then gargled and spat out a mouthful, the way he sometimes saw his father do.

On his way back to the stairwell he stopped at the foreman's desk to look at the Precision Screw calendar. Each month had a different woman. April's had red shoulder-length hair and smiled, a cowboy hat atop her head and a red bandanna around her neck. She wore dungarees and a pale blue blouse through which two huge breasts were faintly visible. Someone had written on the picture, drawing a balloon around the words as in a cartoon: "Boss me around, Hank." Directly below the calendar was a glass ashtray inset in a small black rubber tire. It was filled with butts and ashes. The rest of the desk was a mass of papers and parts, stacked in piles that looked as if they'd come crashing down if bumped even slightly.

Bob had never been left alone on a floor before. Usually his father let him roam only in search of empty soda bottles. If he stopped to look at something, his father would snap at him to keep moving. He'd always wanted to look inside the tar pot at the far end of the floor. He wondered whether he was taking too much time. His father might be trying to check up on him. He ran back to the stairwell and resumed pulling the dirt down the steps, the head of the broom still coming off every now and then.

At the second floor there was a time clock and two doors leading to the outside. It was the workers' entrance, his father said, the way he came in. The bosses came in through another door farther up the side of the building. There were a lot of candy wrappers and cigarette butts on this landing, some stuck to the floor. Bob was picking at one when the noon buzzer went off. The horn was right above his head, and he jumped at the sound of it, sharp and angry like a gigantic bee. After it stopped his ears kept ringing and suddenly he could hear nothing else, not even the sound of the broom against the floor. He wondered whether his father had grown tired of waiting and left him there, alone in the factory.

"Dad?" he shouted. There was no answer. He opened the door to the office waiting room and listened. Nothing. Only the hum of that same machine he'd heard on the fourth floor. So he opened the door to the office and walked in. It was the only carpeted room in the plant. His steps made no noise, but he tiptoed anyway, one step per shadow from the partially shut slats of the venetian blinds. His father did not like him to walk through the office in case Mr. Owens, the boss, was ever there, but this was different. He was worried.

"Dad?" he shouted again. He stood still and listened.

"What do you want?" his father answered. His voice was muffled, and came from somewhere on the other side of the office.

Bob opened the dark green office door, which had a frosted pane of glass with the words "OFFICE: No Admittance" written backward so it could be read only from the outside. It was one of the first things in the plant his father had taught him to read. Directly ahead was another doorway leading into the storage and shipping area where his father worked.

He knew immediately from the smell that his father was inside the office men's room. You needed a key to get in, but he'd seen his father take it many times before. He knocked on the door.

"Entré," his father said. He was sitting on the toilet, his khaki pants draped over his shoes, his shirt and army sweater resting on the roll of flesh around his belly. "You finished?"

Bob shook his head. "One more floor."

"What are you standing here for? Get to work."

Bob watched his father spit on his fingertips and pull the tissues of toilet paper from the dispenser, leaning to one side as he wiped himself. He pulled his pants up, stood, and flushed the toilet all in one motion. Then he stared at Bob.

"What's the big deal?" he said. "Don't you go to the bathroom?"

Bob turned and headed back to the office.

"Wait a second," his father said. "Did you come through the office? I thought I told you never to do that."

"I was worried you'd left."

"Well, I didn't leave. But I just might if you don't shape up. You probably left a mess in there, didn't you?"

Bob shook his head. His father swung the office door open and shook his head.

"See? What did I tell you?"

Across the dark blue office carpet, from the door to the

waiting room to the front door, were his footprints.

"Jesus Christ," his father said. "What a mess. Go ahead, go back through and I'll clean it up. But from now on, don't come through here. Go around through the basement. You understand?"

Bob went back through the office, stepping carefully on each old footprint so as not to make any more. When he got back out to the time clock he decided that the pile of dirt there had to be shoveled into a barrel by the entrance. It was getting too large to move easily. But he'd left the metal dustpan on the fourth floor, and he ran back up to get it.

Bob shoveled five pans of dirt into the barrel, and then decided to sweep the rest down the final set of stairs into the basement. There were no windows on the first floor. The only light after the midway landing was at the foot of the stairs: a single bulb dangling by a long cord.

There were different smells to the dust on the stairs leading down to the basement. It was more stale, and sharper, like the inside of a pickle jar. The wood of the stairs was stained dark from the stuff the workers tracked up. In the basement, there were acid baths for stripping oil off copper blades and brass connectors, and, toward the rear, a paint shop where the gray paint was baked onto the fuse boxes. There were puddles of chemicals and oil, piles of punched metal squares and metal shavings. Everything was sharp or smelly. Sometimes, when his father came in to do the soda machines on Saturdays, there'd be a crew of men working in the basement, and his father would tell him to stay upstairs. Some of the workers were from the local jail, working on a prisoner release program. Others were likely drunk, his father said. "I don't want you near any of those guys when they're working a machine," his father would say. "Someone gets hurt down there every week."

But on Sundays his father would show him how the machines worked. He'd punch out holes in metal, weld a part together on the giant electric welder that once, so his father said, burned a hole right through a man's hand. Sometimes he'd drop a metal basket of dull copper clips that had just been drilled into a vat of green acid, the murky liquid churning and emitting a nose-stinging steam as the metal went under. Then his father pulled them up and tossed them into huge barrels filled with corn cobs ground up like coffee where they'd be tumbled dry and sifted through screens big enough for Bob to walk on. What remained glistened like some precious metal, bright orange-brown clips ready to be sent to the third floor for assembly, and his father would pick up a handful and hold them out, saying, "What do you think of these? Pretty spiffy, huh?"

Bob was getting tired. His arms ached from holding the broom, and his neck was stiff from constantly looking down. He almost wished he hadn't agreed to sweep, that he'd just forgotten about The Neutralizer. But this close to the end, he also felt he had done real work, and that this was the difference between him and Carl, his younger brother, who had to stay at home when his father filled the soda machines.

At last he had pulled the pile of dirt down to the bottom of the stairs, and he ran up to the second-floor landing to get the dustpan. The light coming in through the windows of the workers' entrance hurt his eyes. On the way down, he tried to inspect the stairs, but could barely see them.

They looked clean, except for a cigarette butt, which he picked up and put in the pan. He shoveled up the first pan of dirt and looked for a metal barrel. Even with the single light shining overhead it was dark, and his eyes were not yet completely adjusted after the midday brightness above. He wandered out into the machine shop floor, but couldn't find a barrel.

He thought about dumping the dirt in the dark space beneath the last flight of stairs. But just as he was about to do it, he spotted a barrel. He poured the dirt into it slowly, pretending he was a steam shovel and listening as it landed on the bottom. The metal made the sound louder. As his eyes adjusted, he noticed a lunch bag on the bottom, and he began aiming at it, the paper rattling as the dirt hit. Now he could see the dirt dust rising. Smoke, he imagined. And as he stooped to pick up a second panful, he could hear the paper continuing to rustle from the first bombardment. Only as he approached again did he realize the paper was still making noise. He advanced cautiously toward the barrel. A shape appeared at the edge of the barrel, and paused to screech before hurtling past him. Bob jumped back, the pan flying into the air, junk landing in his hair and on his shirt. He leaned back against a fire door, spitting out dirt and blinking his eyes to clear them. A second black shape was now perched on top of the barrel, its mouth open. It flowed down the barrel faster than a fish in water and scooted by his foot and up the stairs. Now he could see the first rat clearly. It ran into the wall and bounced back, stopping a few steps up from the bottom. Its eyes were white, the color of the outer part of a fried egg. The rat scurried back and forth on the step, and then leapt all the

way down, running back toward the barrel, behind a case
of empty soda bottles at the rear wall behind the stairs.

Bob reached for the broom and held the head end in
front, pushing it slowly along the floor toward the case.
When it touched, he pushed as hard and as fast as he could,
ramming the case against the rat. His feet slipped in the
dirt, and the rat squealed and hissed, squiggling up from
behind and onto the top of the case just as the head of the
broom separated from the handle. Bob took a step back and
looked at the rat, which was turned on its side, its white
eyes twitching and its mouth biting at the air. Then he
swung the broom handle down on the case, breaking a
bottle, again, whacking the wood but missing the rat. He
swung a third time, the blow landing soft on the case, and
he heard one final, slow squeak. He thrust the end of the
handle against the rat, pushing it into the broken bottle,
where its body lodged.

"What's going on down there," his father yelled from
above. He came running downstairs and paused at the last
step. Bob pointed to the rat.

"You little fool," he said. "You should know better than
to mess with a rat." He yanked the broom handle out of
Bob's hands and poked the rat. "It's dead all right. Look at
those eyes—it's blind."

"It wouldn't run away like the other one."

"It couldn't see, that's why."

"It was making noise—I had to hit it."

"You did okay," he said, rubbing Bob's hair. "But you
got this garbage all over you. Here, come with me." He led
Bob to the row of soapstone sinks where the workers
washed up.

"Shut your eyes," he said, pushing Bob's head under the faucet and turning the water on. "Hold your breath."

The spray hit hard, biting, his shirt sinking tight and cold around his back. "You've done good today," his father said. "You did a good job on the stairs and you get a bounty for getting that rat. We'll clean you up and go get that toy."

The water climbed up his nose and stung, filling his eyes with tears. He felt his skin break into goose bumps and he wanted to jerk his head back for air, but he didn't. He kept his eyes shut tight, and his head still in his father's thick hands.

··*Field Work*··

*I*n April Bob started work at Apley's farm after school
let out. He was on the track team but convinced Coach
Medina that the run over to the farm was enough of a
workout. There was nothing the coach could say. It was
that or quit. The team was a joke, so his points in the races
were of no consequence. Medina's only concern was
whether Bob set a bad example for the other members of
the team.

Bob's father said he should stick it out on the team and
hold off working until the summer. "I'll get you a job at the
plant," he promised.

Bob's mother protested. "Apley's good enough to come
through with a job for you, you better take it," she said.
"He said he hadn't been planning to hire anyone this summer, but that since you were family, he'd make an excep-

tion." She turned to his father to emphasize her next words. "That's more than anyone in your family will do for our boys. Besides, it's good work, the farm. A boy should be outdoors."

"Will you cut the crap," Frank said. "Work is work as long as it pays. I don't have anything more to say about it. You want him to work for Apley and his fancy farm, fine. Let him do it and shut up."

Carl ran with Bob to the edge of the farmland, then cut back toward the high school through White's Woods, a nature preserve. Carl agreed to bring home Bob's books and school clothes. Their mother would pick him up at six each evening.

Carl thought Bob was stupid to be taking a job during track season. "You're going to wreck your season," he said. "Your times will never get down to what they could be."

"They'll be okay," Bob said. "This is outdoor work. Physical work. I'll stay in shape, you'll see."

"Will you get any better, though? You won't be able to run with me for as long as I want to work out."

"I don't have to," Bob said. He gave his brother a poke in the chest. "You've got more to do just to catch up with me."

"Yeah, yeah. We'll see."

"We will see." That was the line he was taking. To his father. His brother. Medina. He was sixteen and it was his decision. Making money had become his priority. There was college to save for, things to buy. He had to build a foundation to get the hell away from home. Maybe if the coach was a little more fun or the team a little better he would have done things differently. But as it was, the coach was a cross between a preppy and a Marine drill sergeant. He had a degree from Dartmouth and all the track records in the league, set just four and five years before. Medina's entire training method consisted of vicious repetitions on the track—interval training, he called it—and the workouts left Bob exhausted and brain dead. He was too old to spend his days running in circles.

Apley was tickled that Bob ran to the farm. "You must have a ton of energy," he said. "We'll see if you can keep it up after you work here a few days."

"No problem," Bob said. "It's only three miles."

"You don't know what I've got planned for you, Ace," Apley said. He looked down at Bob's track shoes. "And I'm afraid what you've got on your feet won't do. What's your father wear in that factory?"

"Just regular shoes, I guess," Bob said.

"They must have steel tips in 'em. Even he would think of that, wouldn't he?"

"Yeah, sure. Steel tips." Bob looked at Apley closely. His eyebrows were tensed as if he were squinting, and his lips were drawn tight. There was no way to read his remark.

"I think we've got some old work shoes of Ted's out back. I'll get you those for now. You've got to have work shoes."

Ted's feet were a size larger than Bob's. Apley gave him a pair of thick socks to make up the difference. "Your feet will get hot," he said. "Make sure to bring your own work shoes tomorrow."

Apley led Bob behind the barn and pointed to an old GM truck. Its headlights extended from the hood and were painted half black, a precaution during World War II, Apley told Bob. The rear bed sideboards were weathered gray and rounded at the edges.

"You ever drive anything like this before?" he asked. Without waiting for an answer, he went on. "You've got to double-clutch 'em. Once to get out of gear, again to get into the next gear, no matter whether you're going up or down, forward or reverse. Got it?" He handed Bob the keys.

"Where to?" Bob asked.

"That's the sticky part, Ace," he said. "It's a tough job, but it needs to be done. You up for it?"

"That's what I'm here for, right?" Bob said.

Apley nodded melodramatically, his eyebrows arched, his mouth puckered up. "That's one way of looking at it," he said. "Still, I didn't want to mention the job that needs doing when you said you wanted to work here. It's a killer, this one. But it has to be done every so often."

Apley paused and folded his arms across his chest. It was clear that Apley enjoyed creating a little suspense. Ever since Bob was a boy, he'd heard stories of the pranks Apley pulled on his mother's three brothers when they had worked on the farm. He had stranded Uncle Jason on the roof of the barn by removing the ladder, tied Uncle Kap's car to a tree, causing its bumper to rip off when he drove away, and, on the milk route, left Uncle Bart standing by the road relieving himself of an early-morning overload of coffee. Nothing too mean. Bob was prepared for Apley to pull a stunt at any time.

"Okay," Apley continued. "Every couple of years, when we switch the field on top of the ridge from corn to alfalfa or back again, we clean the rocks out of it. That's what I need you to do."

"Rocks?" Bob wasn't sure how the field could be planted in the first place if it had rocks everywhere.

"You know, rocks," Apley said, winking at him. "Those hard little things that come in different shapes and sizes."

Bob grinned. "Oh, those rocks."

"When they get about yea big"—Apley held up a fist; the veins on the back of his hand bulged, and there was a crescent of dirt wedged beneath his thumbnail—"they begin to dent the tiller and make it hard to lay down the corn seed evenly. I don't think we cleaned it out last when we switched over to alfalfa. I was up there last week, and it looks like we really need to get to it this year."

"Just shovel them into the truck?"

"Not with a shovel, you don't," Apley said. "There's barely enough topsoil up on the ridge the way it is. If we used a shovel on the rocks every time we cleaned them out, we'd be down to ledge now." He bent down and picked a rock off the cow yard. "Here's what you do," he said, tossing it into the back of the truck. It rattled around, scaring a flock of starlings from the top of the silo.

"Hey, boy," someone yelled from the barn window. "Don't you go frightening my girls right before they milk. What's wrong with you?"

Apley elbowed Bob. "He's the new boy, Neugent. My what? Second cousin? The blood's a little diluted on that side of the family. He didn't mean any harm."

Neugent was Apley's barn man. He had been with him for years. His entire family had been raised on the farm and gone off on their own. It was rare for barn hands to hang on this long, but the job was a good one. Bob's mother said that Apley paid him a bonus each year out of the farm's profits. Neugent also lived rent free in a two-story colonial, built in 1792, which was bigger and nicer than the house Bob lived in.

Neugent emerged from the barn, wiping his hands on a rag. His arms were as thick as Bob's legs. "So, Apley, you got more of your family here," he said. "No farmin' instincts in this one, judging from the racket he makes at milkin' time. And glasses, too. I don't know about this one."

"I figure he's got at least half a chance of working out," Apley said.

Apley wasn't grinning. Bob began to resent Apley's remarks. Jokes were one thing. But ever since he had been a boy, he had heard asides like this about his father every time his mother's family got together.

Neugent offered a hand and Bob shook it. Neugent grinned at Apley. "I don't know," he said. "He feels pretty scrawny. You think he can cut it?"

"It's possible," Apley said. "If he's anything like his mother, he's smart as hell."

"Well, Christ, Apley, he don't need brains around here. We'll take care of that. All he's got to do is do."

"We're sending him up to the top field to get the rocks out," Apley said. He checked his watch.

"Oh," Neugent said, nodding. "We'll find out fast enough what he's made of, won't we."

"If we ever get going," Apley said. "C'mon, I'll drive you up there. After that, you're on your own."

Bob watched Apley drive. The shifting didn't appear that difficult. He thought he could manage, although he had driven a standard just once. There was a rhythm to it. With Apley, it was like clockwork: left foot down, right hand forward, left foot up and down again, pause and move it into gear.

Apley turned off the road and edged the truck cautiously past some trees and through a narrow opening in the stone wall. Suddenly the field was visible. Half of it had been recently turned over; the other half was alfalfa, sending up new growth. The field rolled along the top of the ridge for at least several hundred yards. Apley drove along the edge toward the back.

"How big is this?" Bob asked.

"The side you have to get the rocks out of is seven acres. We need to plant in two weeks."

Bob looked out the window at the dirt furrows. He could see an occasional stone, but nothing too bad. "It looks pretty good," he said.

Apley glanced at him and shook his head as he slowed the truck to a crawl and took it out into the dirt. It was soft, and the engine whined in first gear. "When you're out here, don't take it any higher than second," he said. "The ground's wet still, and you could dig yourself a hell of a hole."

Apley brought the truck to a halt on a slight incline and pulled out the parking brake. He hopped out and walked back toward the dirt road. Bob followed.

"C'mere," he said, waving Bob over. "Look close."

Bob walked through the dirt toward Apley. It wasn't what you'd call mud. But you sunk into it anyway. And with each step, there was a stone.

"Take a good look," Apley said. "You'll see what I mean."

Bob did see. There were rocks the size of Apley's fist everywhere, as far as he looked. He couldn't imagine how long it would take. The sound of his own voice surprised him. "Where do they come from?"

Apley shrugged. "From down below, I suppose."

"And it's like this every two years?"

"This might be four years."

"Anything the size of your fist goes?"

Apley nodded solemnly. He bent over and picked one out of the damp soil and wiped off a bit of the dirt clumped to the side. He tossed the stone underhand toward the truck. It thudded dully in the bed. "This needs to be done," he said.

Bob picked a stone out of the soil. It was damp and cool, and he could feel the dirt wedging beneath his fingernails. He shot-putted it over the side of the panels into the truck, and listened to it roll slowly toward the cab.

"If you find anything too big, mark it with a branch and we'll pull it out with a tractor. How you gettin' home?"

"My mother said she'd swing by around six."

"I'll send her up here."

Bob nodded and watched Apley walk off. He cut through a side gate and headed down the slope toward the barn. Two blue jays squawked at him from the bushes, and flew off overhead, one of them dropping a load as it passed. Bob listened to trucks droning along the main road. He could see Neugent revving a tractor in the barnyard. Apley was farther down now, near the hog pen.

It dawned on Bob that he had been standing for five minutes without doing a thing. The whole thing couldn't be real, not a job like this.

Why bother? Why? he was thinking as he tossed stones up. At first he picked whatever he saw out of the muck. Then he got more organized, trying to cover three furrows at a time evenly. He was yet to cover the wooden bed of the truck when he heard a beeping at the far end of the field. He could see his mother's black Volkswagen there. She waved to him. He threw one last rock in the back of the truck. It clacked like one pool ball smacking into another.

Bob couldn't get all the dirt out from under his fingernails. His father said to sit down for supper anyway.

"After dinner, you're going to polish those shoes," his father said. He plopped his coffee cup down emphatically on the table, as if this were the signal to begin arguing.

"Dad, they were a wreck before I even wore them."

"Don't you think you're being a little too fussy?" Bob's mother said. "It's a farm after all." She was tilting a glass of wine on the rim of its base and watching it as it almost spilled.

"Don't give me that, Ellie," he said. "First thing you know, Apley will be talking about this all over town. About how I send my kid to work in sneakers and let him bring back the borrowed shoes caked with mud."

"That's preposterous," she said. "I think it's darn nice of Apley to give Bob a job." The buzzer on the kitchen stove sounded, and she went into the kitchen.

"I didn't say it wasn't. I don't want him talking, that's all."

"Who gives a shit?" Carl said. "Apley's just a goddamn farmer. So what if his family's been in town forever. It's just proof there's no evolutionary development." He rolled his paper napkin in a ball and tossed it at Bob's glass of milk.

"Knock it off," Bob said, throwing the napkin off the wall.

"Both of you knock it off," Bob's father said. "There's nothing else to talk about here. Polish the shoes."

"I don't like the tone of your comments, young man," Bob's mother said to Carl as she carried in a plate of biscuits. She set one on each plate. "With an attitude like that, you'll have a hard time finding a job anywhere, not to mention the farm."

"I wouldn't work at the farm," Carl said, kicking a biscuit across his plate with his index fingers. "Picking rocks out of a field? There's got to be a better way to make a buck."

"And what did you have in mind, miss?" Bob's father said. "Part-time work at the yarn shop up town?"

Bob heard steps overhead. The cellar door swung open. "How about you give these a shine when you finish with those?"

"C'mon, give me a break."

Carl came downstairs. He had a soda for Bob. "I thought you might be thirsty," he said, sitting on a cinder block.

Bob took a long drink. The shoes were almost done. They didn't look very good, just better than they did before he started. There were still fissures of dirt in the creases of the leather that he sealed with polish and buffed with a brush.

"I guess you don't feel like talking," Carl said.

"No, it's not that," Bob said. "I'm just tired."

"Do you really want to work like this? Picking rocks out of a field?"

"It's not forever." He turned the shoes over and looked at the soles again. There was a lot of wear on those soles.

"Seven acres is forever. Coach Medina is worried you won't want to run."

"I'll keep up, you'll see."

"But you'll have a hard time breaking ten minutes in the two mile," he said. "You need more distance work than just running over to the farm."

"I'll run in the morning."

"You're nuts. You won't be able to. Have you even done your homework?"

"I've got some free time in the morning. I'll do it then."

Carl shook his head and stood up. "I don't know about this job shit. There's got to be something easier."

Bob shrugged his shoulders. His brother didn't understand, and that was all right. He never understood. He was always following in the wake of what Bob went through first. Bob experienced it, digested it, and then handed it down to Carl for him to try. If the farm didn't work out, he would learn it firsthand. Then and only then Carl would know for sure. He would have more than some half-ass opinion. He would have the real story.

• • •

Carl was already in sweats and loosening up by the locker room door. "C'mon, Bob," he said. "Let's get moving."

"Yeah, right." He stuck Ted's work shoes with his father's, which fit into a backpack already bulging with dungarees and a blue, long-sleeved workshirt. "I'll warm up as we run."

Carl gave him a "don't-be-a-dope" look, but said nothing. As they ran down the hill from the high school, Carl asked whether the backpack felt funny.

"It's heavy," Bob said. "But it won't be this bad after today. I'll leave the shoes over there." The backpack was also loose. With each step, the shoes whacked against his back. It wasn't long before the pain became a distraction. Carl began to pull away at a pace Bob knew he should have been able to match. Carl looked back once, but Bob waved him on. He lost sight of Carl when he cut into the woods that bordered the farm.

It was no big deal, letting Carl stretch it out in practice once in a while. Even though they'd been running together for only a year, they each knew that there were good days and bad days. Sometimes a hard practice was just impossible. Today was one of those days. The races were all that really counted, and, unless he was injured, Bob always won those.

It was misting. Tiny, perfectly formed drops of water covered his lenses, preventing him from seeing down the dirt road that led to the farm. When he focused on his lenses, he could see a hundred versions of the greens and grays in the swamp on either side of the road through miniature fish-eye effects of the drops. He stopped running. His back was too sore, and with his vision obscured, he worried about getting a stone bruise.

The last stretch of road before the farm passed through a thicket of spruce. There were horse and carriage trails on both sides. The rich folks in town used them all the time. So did a local horse farm. Ahead, a partridge waddled across the road, indifferent to his advance. A catbird in a sassafras sapling permitted him to approach within arm's length until the sound of a truck scared it off. The pickup came up from behind Bob, pulling over just after it passed. Neugent.

"I thought you were running over to the farm," he said from the window. "Get in here, I'll take you there."

Bob jogged up to the truck and hopped in.

"You won't get to work early walking like that," Neugent said. "Christ, you look like one of those rich old ladies from town on a nature walk."

Pulling the truck ahead twenty or thirty yards in first gear was the only thing that gave him a sense of progress. The whiny gargle of the engine turning over startled the blue jays and crows that watched his work from the brush. He never saw them returning. But when he started the engine up every hour or two, they flew off again.

Bob had yet to double-clutch the truck. Apley left it in first with the parking brake on. Bob simply took the brake off and gave it enough gas to inch forward. The rocks rattled around in back, clacking and whacking off the gray sideboards as he rolled across the soft mounds of the field.

The mist gave the dirt a veneer of moisture that turned

into a muddy smear when Bob picked the stones from it. He tried to create a rhythm to the work: stop, stoop, pick, toss, and step. It was no use. His mind wandered anyway. He found himself turned toward the far end of the field, staring at the blurred boundary where the peak of the ridge, mist, and sky merged. He distinguished only the extremes: close to where he stood, the gray of an old stone wall, the lush green of the spring grass alongside the field, and far ahead, where the fog-white mist became a slurry of gray sky. But he couldn't tell where the land ended and the sky began. It was as if a thick bank of clouds had descended over the landscape. This was perfect weather for running. For long distances at slow paces. For watching the mist collect into small drops of moisture along the hairs of your arm.

From this indistinct flow of unwished thoughts, one merging into the next, Bob measured time. Sometimes he would twitch, as if he had been about to fall asleep while standing, and he'd suddenly wonder whether he'd been doing anything at all, whether an hour or more had passed since he'd last added another stone to the growing pile in the back of the truck. But no matter how fast he worked, the pile seemed to grow at the same slow rate. That part of the field that remained to be done seemed to be expanding. He attributed this perception to fatigue. There were so many rocks, he couldn't believe the field had been picked any time recently. He wondered whether it had ever been done.

Bob tried to imagine what he was earning per rock. He was probably tossing ten per minute. At four dollars an hour, that meant each stone was worth one-half cent. That was a terrible price for piece work. He was glad that he was earning an hourly wage—it gave the job a more professional feel.

Every time he checked his progress, he spotted at least as many overlooked stones as he'd already picked and tossed. He wondered whether they had been invisible from the direction he'd worked, or had lodged on the far side of a furrow, or had been obscured by mud. But when he walked back to get them and returned to the truck, he would find more—all different. Even through the mud he could see there were many different types of rock: porphyry, granite and feldspar, gneiss, schists, and small, smooth, rounded pieces of quartzite. He thought of the ceaseless flaking of bedrock and percolation upward of its particles, year by year, decade after decade. He wondered how long it took and whether some of the rocks he held this afternoon had begun that journey upward when his father was his age and playing ball at the Community Field diamond three miles away.

The shape of a man walking through the mist startled him. It was Apley. He hadn't heard the truck, although he could see the pickup Neugent had driven at the gateway of the field.

"How's it going, Ace?" Apley said from a distance. He picked up a stone with this left hand and tossed it toward a squawking crow a couple of hundred feet away. It crashed a few feet below the crow in the tree at the side of the field. The crow flew off, squawking still. Apley had a strong arm.

"Well?" he said when he got to where Bob was working.

Bob couldn't say a word. This was too much. To expect he'd like working in a field like this, that was too much to ask. "I'm getting there," he said.

Apley shook his head as if he'd just witnessed some small but distasteful incident. It was the way parents shake their heads when they see another parent slap a cranky kid in the supermarket. "It's a terrible job," he said. "Just a rotten way to start out here. But it needed to be done. Keep at it."

Apley walked over the part Bob had done, picking up a stone here and there and throwing it to the side. Bob kept on with his path. Of course there were stones he'd missed. How could there not be?

When Apley returned, he had a stone in hand and was tossing it up and down like a baseball. Bob stood, aware that his dungarees were caked with mud from wiping his hands. This is it, he thought. I'm getting the "can't-you-do-a-simple-job-right" lecture.

"What is this?" Apley said.

"A stone I missed, I guess," Bob said.

Apley looked at the stone, then at Bob. "I thought your mother said you were smart. I know it's a stone. I meant, what kind of stone? She said you knew rocks."

Bob looked at it. He took it from Apley's hand. It was too dense to be granite or some other kind of common bedrock. It was definitely an ore. He picked at it, scraping off some of the mud. It didn't even look like a rock. And there was rust on it.

"Ever see anything like that?" Apley asked.

"I'm not sure this is a rock," Bob said. "It's heavy like iron ore, but it looks like pure iron."

"Well, I'll be," Apley said. "You do know your rocks. It's an old ox shoe. Ever see one? They used to shoe oxen like horses. They'd keep a fire going by the side over there. You can still find the spot in the stone wall where they'd hammer out a new one whenever an ox lost one. This one here looks like a reject someone tossed into the field. Want it?"

"I don't think so."

"Good," he said, throwing it into the bushes. "If you want a good one, you can probably scrounge around in the bushes over there with a shovel. Antique shops sell them as paperweights."

"I'll make a point to look for one," Bob said.

When Bob rolled out of bed on Friday morning, he had trouble standing straight. His lower back was stiff and hurt as if something the size of a tennis ball had been inserted in between his vertebrae. He thought he was in good shape from running, but the muscles he used for working were all different from those used for track.

A hot shower didn't help much, so he got down on the living room rug and went through a regular loosening-up sequence.

Carl was up. On his way to the shower, he watched Bob for a few seconds, rubbed his eyes, and said, "That job is screwing you up. You shouldn't be like this."

"I'm all right," Bob said. "You'll see this afternoon."

"I hope. I hope you're not shot. Are you going to feel like running with me on Sunday? I want to run in White's Woods. If you're not going to run with me, will you drive me there?"

"I'll run on Sunday, don't worry about it."

But while Carl was in the shower, Bob found he couldn't open a new jar of jam. His hands and fingers were too sore

and tired from picking the rocks. It made him think twice
about Sunday. He had to hold the jar under hot water in
the kitchen sink, provoking Carl to yell from the shower
that the water had gone cold. He could barely open it. As
he waited for his toast, he watched their old Lab limping
up the driveway. The dog was going to get hit crossing the
road sooner or later. They all knew it.

Bob never planned to think about anything during a race.
But for a while, during the initial laps of the two mile, he
found himself daydreaming. This race was no different. A
Woodbury runner was setting the pace. But he wasn't the
school's best. Carl went after the guy and stayed on his
shoulder. Bob stayed on Carl's shoulder, and checked for a
sign from Medina at the quarter mile. He gave Bob the
thumbs-up.

Woodbury was Medina's high school. So this race was
more important to him than any other. The meet itself was
hopeless. His old coach at Woodbury, Bumps, he called
him, was still there, and there was a certain amount of
showing off before his running mentor. Showing off in a
classy way was important to Medina. He drove an MG and
had a girlfriend at Yale Law School who'd gone to Smith.
Bob figured that was standard issue at Dartmouth, along
with a little green hooded sweatshirt and a dry, sarcastic
laugh. His girlfriend usually came up for their Friday afternoon meets and sat in a lawn chair knitting and cheering.
"Hooray," she yelled.

Woodbury usually had good runners. This year, though,
there was just an okay runner, Rider Brindle. His team-

mates called him "Stitch." He had beaten Bob and Carl in cross country the previous fall. But they had worked hard over the winter and had beaten Brindle easily in the first invitational track meet of the spring.

Bob was thinking about this when Brindle made his move after they went through the mile at 5:03. A good pace, but nothing great. Brindle kicked out about fifteen yards ahead of the field. Medina yelled to stay with him.

"Don't lose contact," he said. "Carl, Bob, go get him."

Carl kicked up after him and Bob followed. When he got to Carl's shoulder, he said, "Don't push it, he'll die." Carl's eyes met Bob's for a second, then he turned his head toward Brindle. Carl's look told Bob that he thought Bob was nuts.

Carl pushed on toward Brindle, whose lead was only about five yards now. Bob hung back at about ten yards. At the sixth lap, Medina said, "Smart, Bob. Now take him."

Some runners fade in a race. They never lose form or character, they simply fall farther and farther behind. But their heads remain up, their stride even and constant, albeit slower and shorter. Other runners lose form but summon a will that supersedes aesthetics. With half-dried spit caked to their faces, they flail toward the finish line, heaving and victorious, immediately to collapse and vomit. Today, Bob was the poorer combination of both, a fading runner gone spastic, gasping, his leaden legs nearly tripping over the slightest variations of the track's surface, his vision spotty and his arms pumping crisscross as if he were in some liquid-filled nightmare running from a great boy-eating beetle.

"Pick it up, Bob, get going," Medina yelled in his ear at the start of the final lap. He knew this was simply a form of mental cruelty, the type Medina delighted in. There was no chance for him. He'd merely try to hang on to third for the points, although feeling as he did he really couldn't give a shit. Brindle and Carl were fighting it out halfway across the field. Too bad. Carl didn't have a kick. Bob could guess the outcome. He'd have to concentrate on finishing the race without collapsing.

As he rounded the final bend, he tried to put a little extra effort into it, but it was no use. His body had quit long before. He found himself thinking about track, about how stupid it was to run in a circle, over and over, over and over, and then the Woodbury runner who'd led early was by him. By him so easily there was no point in fighting. The guy wasn't even breathing hard. Or so it seemed. Anything was easier than the way he was breathing.

Later, as Bob lay on his back in the infield, Medina stood over him, clipboard in hand, his blond hair fluffing up slightly in the wind. "You punked out," he said nonchalantly, a pencil tip posed thoughtfully at his lip. "If you don't work out with the team next week, you're off it."

When Apley handed Bob a small manila envelope containing four twenty-dollar bills and some singles, it wasn't a hard decision to make. Apley had shaken his hand when he paid him, and told Bob that he was doing a good job. A tough one, too, he said.

While Bob waited for his mother, he looked at the pay envelope. On one side, in pencil, were the days he'd worked, and the hours per day. Three each weekday and six on Saturday. Twenty-one in all. These numbers looked much better than even the best quarter splits from an interval workout. And six hours was a generous figuring of how long he'd been there on Saturday. This work stuff was all right. A great secret among men, the way time could be turned into money. No mind that his hands ached and his arms quivered from fatigue. This was what counted. When Bob succeeded in double-clutching the truck out of the field and across the street to where Apley had told him to dump the load, he found a gully filled with mounds of field stones, thousands and thousands of them. Bob tossed his stones out, shoveled them out, heaved handfuls, and they rolled down against a century's worth of field pickings, clack, clack, clack, knocking down the water plants and ricocheting into saplings. His rocks, there with all the others.

·· *Night Work* ··

*T*he raccoons were taking the corn crop to hell. Apley
estimated that they had wrecked two acres in one field
alone. They knocked the stalks over to get at the ears. At
harvest, the debris would jam the machinery.

"Those coons have already added a day of field work,"
Apley said. "It's never been this bad before."

Simp, the new barn hand, agreed.

Bob leaned against Apley's pickup. Since it was his first
summer on the farm, he didn't have anything to compare
it to.

"Yep," Simp went on. "Those coons are something."

Apley ignored Simp. You had to work for a while on the
farm before your opinion counted for something. And
Simp wasn't off to a good start. He and his family were
down from Maine, where his potato farm had been repos-

sessed. He replaced Neugent after Neugent got hurt. During his first week, he put a prize bull that Apley had rented for just seven days in a field without any heifers. By the time Apley figured it out, it was too late. The bull was booked all summer and had to be returned. All Simp could say for himself was that he didn't know there were two different fields south of the highway. That made sense to Bob, but Apley hadn't bought it.

"What do you think, Ace?" Apley asked.

"I guess we've got to keep them out of the corn," he said.

Apley had on his poker face. Bob couldn't tell what he was thinking, but he suspected there was a bad job in the works.

"Maybe we could set up some pans and spoons to flap in the breeze," Bob said. "Scare 'em away."

"Those aren't rabbits or woodchucks, Ace," Apley said. "Besides, I don't want that field looking like a used car lot."

Simp snorted, slapping his hands on his thighs.

"I think we've got to sit up there all night," Apley said.

"Yeah," Simp said. "That's it. With a gun, too."

Apley glanced at Simp. "You can shoot, can't you, Ace?"

Bob nodded, and Apley patted him on the back.

"That's the way to handle it," he said. "You agree?"

"Sure," Bob said. What else could he say? Apley had hired him to do odd jobs around the farm. This was an odd job.

Simp aimed a make-believe rifle. "Kaboom," he said, his arms jolting up in recoil. "See, Bob. It's not that tough."

"You want me there all night?" Bob asked.

Apley was quiet for a second. "If you can stop them by sitting up there just part of the night, power to you."

Simp opened his mouth wide as if he were about to belly
laugh. "More likely, though," he said, "you'll need to patrol
that whole field. They're sneaky little things, coons are.

"Simp," Apley added, "since you know a bit about coons,
you can take over for Bob at three."

"Three in the morning?" Simp asked.

"That's what I said. Then come in and milk the herd. I'll
clean up the barn and put down the lime so you can catch
a nap before afternoon chores."

"Oh, man," Simp said, heading into the barn. "At three?
What is Linda going to say about this?"

Bob had parked his mother's Volkswagen at the entrance
to the field. The sun had gone down, but there was still
light enough to make out the shapes of things. It was the
same field he'd taken all the stones out of in the spring. But
filled with corn it looked completely different—as dense
and endless as the sea. The corn rolled along the top of the
ridge as far as Bob could see, and even though the muggy
air seemed motionless to him, the leaves of the plants were
moving ever so slightly, as if brought to motion by the heat
of their own growth, filling the night air with a steady
whisper of friction. He'd have a hard time staying awake
to a sound like that.

Bob had taped a flashlight to his .12 gauge to jack the
coons if and when they came. As far as he was concerned,
this wasn't sport. The sooner he scared them off, the better.

There was a half-moon rising. As the glow of sunset
faded, it gave off enough light for Bob to pick a spot away
from the thick poison ivy that ran along the stone wall. He

could hear a couple of whippoorwills in the swamp behind him. From where he sat, he could see the lights of Apley's kitchen. His wife, Trudy, was probably just cleaning up. Apley ate late, the way old money always does. The farm-house lights went out right at eleven. The bug repellent with which Bob had drenched himself had worn off. The mosquitoes were biting. But he didn't slap at them. He was afraid the sound would scare off the coons. Instead, he waved his hands in one continuous motion, gun across his lap. Three in the morning seemed a long way off.

Finally, he heard movement in the brush from the swamp behind the field. Leaves rustled, twigs cracked. He gradually recognized it was no coon. Too big and clumsy.

When a shape popped into the field a few yards away, Bob flicked on the light and aimed. It was Simp. He was carrying a small rifle, a .22 Bob guessed.

"What the hell are you doing, Simp?" Bob hissed. "I almost shot you."

"Take it easy, there, young one," he said, speaking in a daytime voice. "I was driving the coons to you."

"What? They aren't deer. You can't drive a coon."

"Now, how can you say that?" Simp said. "How do you know?"

Simp was staring at him, wearing a blue T-shirt that said, "Live your tradition. Visit Sturbridge Village."

Bob clicked off the light. It was only midnight. He wanted to know why Simp had come early.

"Couldn't sleep," he said. "Linda is pissed at me for letting Apley get me into this. She thinks a husband be-longs in bed at night."

Simp was still speaking loudly. At night in a field, talk

seems much louder. Bob was afraid that Apley might hear him all the way back at the house. "Let's take a couple of spots, then," Bob said, whispering, "two good spots, and finish this job tonight."

"That's right, let's get it done," Simp said, keeping the volume up. "Although to speak the truth, I could use a few nights away from Linda. When I was your age, I couldn't imagine there was such a thing as too much nooky. Let me tell you, though, and this is the God's truth, there is."

Bob tugged on the flashlight to make sure it was snug. If he had to choose between being bitten by mosquitoes for three hours more or listening to Simp talk about his sex life, he was ready to go.

"Of course, you're probably not at that stage yet, are you?" Simp said. "What are you, anyway? Seventeen? Eighteen?"

"Sixteen," Bob whispered.

"What?"

"Sixteen." This time, Bob spoke normally. It was no use.

"Sixteen? Then you got something to look forward to. Heck, no sense in me telling you all this. You see, at my age, it's all downhill. Maybe I used myself up screwing around at an early age. Drained the batteries, if you get my drift. There ain't much else to do in Maine during the winter. I keep telling Linda, 'Hey, give this man a rest.' "

Bob walked a few steps off. Simp kept on talking, getting louder. "Your first job?" he asked.

"My first real job," Bob said.

"You picked a good one. You'll learn a lot here. Apley's tough. I could have told you that right away. Most bosses after this will be easy compared to him."

"He's fair, though," Bob said. He guessed Simp didn't know Apley was his second cousin.

"Oh yeah, he's fair. But this bit about liming the barn—give me a break. It's a barn, for chrissake."

"It's always been that way."

"It's too fussy for a farm, take it from Simp."

"Maybe that's why the farm has been in the same family for a hundred years. It has a reputation."

"That's it, isn't it? That's a real Connecticut thing, your reputation and so on."

"It's not that big a deal. What's it take? Fifteen minutes to lime the barn?"

"It's not the time, Bob. You'll learn that soon enough. It's the point of it. What is the point?"

"I guess I don't see your point."

"Apley's got a boy, doesn't he? A man now. And where the hell is he? That's the point, dammit. He doesn't want this shit."

Bob looked at Simp. He was pushing the dirt at his feet with the rifle butt. They'd probably already scared the coons away for the night. Bob knew there was no sense in arguing with a man like Simp, but he couldn't help it.

"Ted might be back yet," Bob said. "When he and his wife, Chase, were here in July, he said he was getting sick of stock cars."

"No way. Once they leave the farm, they never come back. That's why a man like me never has to worry about work. Even with all the farms shutting down today. And you know why? 'Cause you can't find a professional barn man anymore. That's what makes me so valuable."

"Give me a break, Simp."

"Naw, I'm serious." He struck a match to check his watch, and tossed it over his shoulder without snuffing it.

"Simp, watch the matches."

"You give me a break," he said. "Don't bust on me. Between Linda and Apley, I've got enough bones up my ass without you."

"Sorry, Simp." Bob stood up to take another position. But Simp grabbed him by the pant leg.

"Take a seat," he said. "Don't leave just yet. Tell me a little bit about yourself. What are your plans. College?"

"Yeah, college."

"That's good. Real good. But I'll tell you something. There's a lot of college graduates without jobs. You might have something right here. With Apley's kids out of the way, you and me could make Apley an offer for this place. Heck, what's the point of hanging on to it? Might as well sell it to a couple of guys who know the place like us."

"Simp, let's discuss this later," Bob said. "Because if we don't get those coons, we won't have jobs to speak of."

"I like that," Simp said. "Right you are. Back to work. See you here at three."

Bob took a position halfway up the other side of the corn field, close to where the damage was worst. He'd looked at it earlier in the day. The corn stalks were knocked over like someone had driven a jeep into the field.

Bob didn't enjoy sitting in a field waiting for the coons to come. He imagined how his parents would talk about it. His father: "If there's a buck in it, do it." His mother: "If Apley tells you to do it, do it." A quick buck versus duty. It was the story of the two families, his father's and his mother's. The schemers against the corporate warriors.

Only both of them fell short. And beyond all this, Bob knew that if he wasn't there to do it, Apley would probably be here himself. He was always working as hard as anyone else. That's what made it tough to resent being given a bad job.

A faint breeze moved through the corn field, rattling the leaves lightly as if a rain shower had started. An owl hooted in the woods, and all of a sudden Bob had the feeling that something was happening. First the breeze, then the hoot. He began to feel they were signs. He could imagine a brigade of coons moving in, as if in a children's book, directing the breeze and the birds to make sounds to cover their noise. He could imagine them silently taking the corn down from right in front of him while he sat there powerless, lulled into a stupor by some animal rite of magic. He could even imagine one fat old coon rocking from side to side as it chugged up to him to nip the tip of his big toe.

Bob jumped. It was three. He didn't know whether he'd dozed off. The last he'd noticed, it had been one-thirty. He thought about cutting across the field, but was worried that Simp might start shooting at any movement in the corn. So he took the long way around and looked for signs of coons. There were none.

When Bob got back to where he'd left Simp, there was no one in sight. "Shit," he said. "That jerk left me."

A branch cracked overhead. "Fooled ya!"

Bob shined his flashlight up. Simp was in the tree. "Simp," he said, "I think it's the coons that are supposed to get treed."

"Never mind how I hunt a coon," he said. "Think results, boy. Results are what count in this world."

• • •

The results weren't too good. When Bob got to the farm the next morning, Apley wanted to see him right away. He had already been up to the field and found another hundred plants down.

"What were you two doing all night?" he said. There was no joking around to this. Apley was mad, and that worried Bob.

"I left at three, and walked around the whole far end on my way out. Nothing had happened up there."

Apley arched his brow and pulled a toothpick from his mouth. "This kind of pisses me off," he said. "Simp swears he didn't sleep a wink. And you swear there was nothing before three. I don't figure it. How could a coon knock down that much corn without being heard?"

It wasn't one of those questions a boss wants answered. Any explanation would come off like a pathetic excuse. So Bob stood there quietly, watching Apley stare at him. He felt like Apley was about to say something really nasty. Maybe another crack about his father. Instead, he put his hand on Bob's shoulder and walked him around the corner of the barn.

"Take a bucket of white paint from the shed and go over to Neugent's house," he said, pointing to where Simp's family lived. "There's a stain on the wall by the back door stairs. Looks like that woman threw coffee grounds on it."

You could tell Simp wasn't inclined to take care of a house. Neugent had lived there for fifteen years, and the lawn was always mowed, the flower patch weeded, and the yard clean. But now you could forget the flower patch.

Then there was the lawn. Bob had been over twice to mow it. The second time, Apley had him ask Simp if the lawn mower in the garage was broken. "What is this?" Simp said. "A friggin' country club? Jeez."

Simp's three boys were in a playpen on the back porch. The oldest looked about five and could easily have climbed out. But he didn't. He stood with his hands on the bars, watching Bob. There was a lollipop in the corner, covered with hornets. Bob shooed them off and tossed the pop into the garbage.

"How you guys doing?" Bob asked, rubbing the hair of the oldest boy. They all kept their mouths shut. Not even a grin. "Okay, where's your mom?"

Again, nothing.

Bob opened the screen door and leaned in. "Hello? Anyone home?"

"Who's that?" Simp said. He was upstairs. "Who's here?"

The ceiling creaked directly overhead. Linda was saying something he couldn't quite make out. Simp was at the head of the stairs. "In a minute," he was saying to her. "Keep your shirt on. Jeez."

Simp came downstairs, a bed sheet wrapped around him like a Roman toga. "Hi," he said. "Linda's up napping with me. The kids all right?"

"Sure." Bob felt a little embarrassed to see Simp. There were dark bags under his eyes, and he had a little snake tattooed in green ink on his shoulder. "I've got some painting to do out back. Just wanted you to know."

"Oh, yeah. That spot there. Good. Apley said something about that." He coughed a couple of times and wandered over to the sink and shifted a few dirty dishes to one side, finding a red plastic cup and filling it with water. He drank it straight down and was breathing heavy. Melon seeds fell from the cup's bottom. The kitchen stank of rotting fruit. "Apley tell you the coons got into the field?"

Bob nodded. He was about to say something when he heard Linda coming down the stairs. She had on a yellow terry cloth robe and had a mask like the Lone Ranger's pushed up over her forehead. Its eye holes were covered with black masking tape. She was a heavy woman. The two of them were like Mutt and Jeff.

"Bob, be a good boy and let Simp get back to bed with me," she said. "C'mon, Simp, upstairs."

"Comin'," Simp said. He followed her up the stairs. "I don't know how those coons did it. I was there all night. Right there."

"Will you hush up about those stupid coons?" Linda said. "Who cares if some corn's gone?"

"See you later," Bob said, letting the screen door slap shut so they'd know he was out. He had this image of her working away like some fleshy piston below Simp, her mask pulled down over her eyes, Simp spread loosely over her like a dog in the back of a pickup on a bumpy road.

The stain was a dark brown splatter mark. There were coffee grounds stuck to the boards, and he scraped them off with his fingernails. He shook up the paint and popped the lid off with a screwdriver. He soaked the brush up thick with white paint and slapped it over the stain. Stroke by stroke it grew fainter, first a bruise, then a blemish, until finally it had disappeared behind a field of uniform white.

• • •

Simp wandered into the field at midnight, his irregular walk visible in the moonlight, rifle over the shoulder, the Sad Sack of professional barn hands.

"Hey, Bob," he said, yawning as he spoke. "You did a good job out back on that stain."

"Thanks. You know, if you want to catch some sleep, I'm doing fine. I'm planning to be here all night."

"Naw," he said. "You don't need to do that. Heck, you're still growing."

"I've got a thermos of coffee. Want some?"

"No, thanks. Brought my own stimulants." He pulled out a pint of whiskey and took a pull from it, smacking his lips just like a kid finishing a glass of milk. "You heard I slept through the chores this afternoon?"

"Yeah. Too beat to wake up, huh?"

"The alarm went off. Next thing I know Apley's downstairs. I don't know what the hell happened. Just rolled over and bam! Right out."

"Apley was upset."

"He really chewed my ass out. About the coons, the chores, the lawn, the stain on the wall, the garbage in the sink. You'd think this place was some sort of national treasure."

"It's been in the same family long enough to make a person particular about appearances." Bob couldn't stand the sound of his own voice defending old money and old land.

"It's not just that, though," Simp said. He took another swig. "It's 'Neugent didn't do that,' or 'Neugent never forgot this.' Christ, I didn't knock him off the truck."

Bob threw his coffee on the ground. "I was doing the best

I could, too, you know. I didn't want him to fall." It had
been Bob's first haying on the farm. He was driving the old
GM truck and got it hung up on some ledge with Neugent
in back on top of a stacked load of hay. Everything went
over. Neugent cracked three vertebrae in his back, ending
his days on the farm. To top it off, Apley's insurance company dropped him after twenty-three years. One accident.
It was the last thing Bob felt like discussing. But when he
started walking off, Simp called out.

"Hey, Bob, I didn't mean it like that. Not that way. It's
just I can't help thinking about all of this. How Apley's kids
took off on him. How Neugent got hurt. And you, too. You
don't know a heck of a lot about a farm, either."

"No, I don't. But I try to do what I'm asked. I try to do
the job."

"Sure, you do," he said. "And you're learning twice as
fast as I could. You're smart. But walk a mile in my shoes.
Just try it."

Bob looked at Simp's shape in the dark and shuddered.
He didn't want Simp's shoes. Not now. Not ever. But there
was the sense that at its worst, his life might be only one
bad break away from Simp's. Say he didn't go to college.
Say he fell off a truck. What would he do? Who would
he be?

"Shit," Simp said. "The bank shuts me down up north.
I got three kids and a woman to support and I'm down here
on a farm with no experienced help and all I get is a load
of shit. Apley's barkin' at me every time I turn around. And
for what? For not liming the barn? Shit, I know how to run
a barn. But this? This is nuts. But I got to take it. Because
I need a job. So I got to figure out some way of making do.

Because I'm the man. Where does it say the man is the one and only? I'm telling you, sometimes it doesn't pay to be a man."

Bob tried to think of something sympathetic to say. But when Simp poured some of the whiskey on his hands and began slapping it over his neck, Bob instead found himself saying, "What the hell are you doing?"

"It'll keep the bugs off—something I learned in Maine. Heck, up there, the bugs are twice as big."

"Yeah, they call 'em bar flies."

"Hey, that's pretty good, Bob. You got a way with words. You probably ought to be a banker and leave this farm for me."

When Bob got back to his spot, he saw the damage of the previous night. It was considerable. There had to be quite a few coons, and no way for Simp not to have heard them. Especially with the air as still as it was. In the swamp, he could hear the whippoorwill and the whistling laugh of woodcock. Far off, a dog barked. Every once in a while there was a high-pitched gritty sound. Bats, he assumed, although he couldn't see any overhead, where the half-moon was so bright it made his eyes hurt.

Sitting by the stump, he was conscious not just of hearing these things, but of the act of hearing, of being so aware he could feel the small methodical action of his own heart. He could imagine this awareness as a field of receptivity, as a radar just outside of which the coons lolled beneath the dark blue spruce of the swamp, chubbing against one another like soft pool balls, joking in coon talk, giggling about Simp and him, slowly queuing to punch in for another night's work. With this, Bob no longer knew whether he was watching the field, or only dreaming that he was. He held his hand in front of his face and stared at it. It seemed pale and distant. It could have been any hand. A dead man's. His. He couldn't say for sure. He concluded he was awake, but too sleepy to continue.

After he'd said good night to Simp and apologized for not being able to stick it out, he felt relieved to be driving back home at three in the morning. To stay awake, he rolled down the front windows and let the night air beat against his face. As he drove up the hill to where his home was, the headlights caught the red eyes of a coon beside the road. It turned and scuttled slowly off into the woods. He gave the car some gas, and then cut the engine and lights, coasting the last hundred yards into his driveway. The front light had been left on for him. He tiptoed out of the car, past the dog asleep on the front steps.

"Some watchdog," he said.

Her tail quivered momentarily, and then she was back asleep.

Inside, he sat in the dark at the kitchen table. He could hear his father snoring down the hall. The house was his now. But he didn't want it. There was no drawer he could open, no paper he could find that he cared to read. Mom and Dad could have it all. It was theirs forever, the little secrets and boxes of photos, their bills and their dreams. Instead, he decided to satisfy the hunger he felt all of a sudden, and opened the refrigerator door. The chilled air fell over his legs and felt good. There was a huge, freshly made cake sitting on a plate directly in front of him. He took it out, intending to have only one slice. But when he began eating it, he couldn't stop. Vanilla cake, coconut icing—his favorite. He finished a quarter of it before he went to bed.

His mother shook him awake at nine.

"Time for work," she said. "Did you get the coon?"

He leaned forward on his elbows. The daylight was blinding. "I don't know," he said. "Maybe. Not while I was there."

"You ate a quarter of the cake, though," she said. "You could have been more considerate. It's for your grandmother's birthday."

"Shit, Mom, I'm sorry."

"Well, forget it. I'll make another. You get home on time tonight, though. Do a good day's work."

That was tough. His sleep was out of whack. He felt foggy-headed and lethargic. He hoped he'd be left alone for a while when he got to the farm, just to give his head a chance to clear. But Apley was standing at the dairy doorway waving him over as he drove in.

"What the hell happened up there last night?" he said, striding toward the car as Bob climbed out.

"What do you mean?" Bob said, trying to think of something to calm Apley down. He already suspected the worst.

"There are more plants down. On the side you were watching, according to Simp."

"There were no coons when I left at three."

"Simp says you were tired and left at two. Did you fall asleep?"

"No," he said, angry at the thought of Simp saying that to Apley. "And I didn't get home till three-thirty. My mom can tell you that." Bob didn't know whether or not he was telling the truth. It might have been the truth. He hadn't even checked the clock when he got home. Unless his mother had been awake without saying a word, she wouldn't know, either. But he was pretty sure Apley wouldn't bother his mom about it.

"What's the use?" Apley said. "Simp swears he was awake. But he came in this morning smelling like whiskey, and I figure he just drank himself asleep up there. Was he into it when you saw him?"

Bob thought about trying to stick up for Simp a bit. To tell Apley about the way Simp was slapping the whiskey around his neck. But that would sound even worse. For both of them.

"Naw," he said. "I didn't see Simp with a bottle. Not when I left."

"Probably hid it." Apley put his hands on his sides and kicked a pebble across the driveway. "Oh, well. We try again tonight, and if the coons don't stop, we're going to make some changes. You go home early and get plenty of sleep."

Bob's mother felt bad for him and made a big dinner to go along with Oma's birthday. His grandmother sat in a chair in the living room asking how the farm was these days, and Bob said, fine, fine, fine to everything she asked.

Bob's father had second thoughts about a big dinner. "That's the last thing he needs," he said. "A gut full of food when he has to stay awake all night."

"You can take a nap after supper," she said to Bob. "Judg-

ing from the way you ate when you got home last night,
you were starving."

"Yeah," Bob said. He knew his father was right, though.
"I've got to make sure I'm there all night tonight. No sleep.
I can't believe he let this happen."

"He sounds like what we used to call white trash," Bob's
mother said. "I'm surprised Apley bothered to hire him.
You can tell the type most of the time. I see them at the
hospital, you know." She took a sip of sherry and looked
across the table at Bob's father. "And at the plant."

"Who cares whether he's trash or not," Bob's father said.
"The point is, you got to stay awake and make sure you do
your part of the job. I have a hunch Apley might show up
tonight just to check on you two."

"It sounds like something Apley would do, dear," Oma
said, nodding. "He can be pretty tricky when his dander's
up."

Bob's mother shook her head, swallowing sherry as she
did. "Not Apley. That's not his way. He tells you to do a
job and expects it to be done. If it isn't, that's another
thing."

"He's a businessman, Ellie," Bob's father said. "And
with a worker like Simp, he needs to check up more often.
That's the bottom line."

Bob's mother was still shaking her head when Bob stood
to clear his plate. "I'm going to rest a bit before dark," he
said. There was no way he was going to get in between a
discussion about what kind of man, farmer, or businessman
Apley was, although he personally felt his mother was
right. Apley wouldn't check. He was smart, but he cut
everyone a lot of slack, too. As if there were some honor

involved with a job. It was like saying, "Let's not kid ourselves. You're a respectable man and so am I. So do your
job and I won't be a prick." It was a great philosophy if you
had the money. Apley had it. The problem came with the
assumption of responsibility. The idea that an individual
was responsible for his actions. For consequences. For
doing what needed to be done. There were times when
things conspired against you and prevented you from living up to the faith Apley put in you. Bob had first sensed
it the day Neugent fell out of the truck. The coons were
almost as bad, slinking into the field without being seen.
Even if Simp had fallen asleep or had been drinking till he
was out of it, those coons knew enough to wait until Bob
left and Simp's eyes were shut. They were like the Fates,
and through their actions they were changing the course of
affairs for Simp and his family, and maybe for Bob himself.
Sometimes, you were going to lose no matter what you did.
Bob's father seemed to know this. His mother didn't. And
Bob could understand both points of view.

Simp showed up a few minutes after Apley's lights went
out. He must have been watching for them. Along with his
.22, he had two burlap sacks slung over his shoulder. There
was a plan.

"Today was garbage day in town," he said. "Linda noticed when she was up there."

"Yeah," Bob said. "How's that going to help?"

"I'm getting to that, Bob. Give the man a chance. You
see, they dump all that garbage at the landfill by Apley's
brother, right? Up near that auto junkyard."

"Yeah, the dump."

"With fresh garbage today, there's bound to be a million coons over there, right? We go over and bag a few, bring 'em back here, and when those swamp coons see their dead comrades, they'll hightail it outta here, right? And we tell Apley we shot the ones we put here. Which we did, right?"

Bob held his breath to avoid laughing. He didn't want to make a big issue out of this with Simp.

"Don't tell me an animal as smart as a coon isn't scared to find its own kind dead."

Bob shook his head slowly.

"This is serious, Bob. You got to go along with me, please. I've been up here all night both nights. Linda's ready to leave me. And I swear I haven't slept. Not a wink. But when you're all alone in the dead of the night, who's to say whether you're awake or asleep. I can't take another chance. Not tonight."

"Simp—" Bob could understand Simp's desperation. But this scheme was out of the question. "You can't try something like this on Apley. Not him."

"Think about it from my point of view, Bob. Think about me, with a family. I've got to get Apley off my back. Got to. I might leave anyway. But I'd like to leave on my own terms."

"Apley won't fall for it."

Simp let a long, deep breath pass through his lips. "Okay, Bob. You're a boy. If it bothers you, that's fine. But at least let me borrow your car. I'll take full responsibility if I get caught. I'll say I clubbed you or something. I don't know."

Even as Bob reached into his pocket for the car keys, he knew what he was going to do. Maybe it was the way Simp called him a boy. Maybe it was just the fact that Simp said he'd take full responsibility. Maybe it was just for the hell of it.

"I'm going," he said to Simp.

Simp's teeth looked like a skeleton's in the moonlight. "Goddamn," he said. "Now I know things are going to turn out all right. I knew you'd understand."

But Bob didn't understand. He couldn't imagine what he'd tell his parents if he was caught. And as he shut off the engine and lights of his mother's VW to coast by Apley's house around midnight, he felt that he was somehow altering the course of his life. For what or to what he couldn't say.

When Simp offered him a sip of whiskey, Bob gladly took it. It tasted awful, but once it hit his stomach, it felt good. He took another swig and handed the bottle back to Simp. As the car rolled onto the pavement, he turned the key and gave the engine some gas, causing it to burst into a high-pitched giggling whine that he revved into order. Throwing the car into gear, he jubilantly headed toward the town dump.

They found the gate to the landfill locked shut. Simp climbed over the fence before Bob could think what to do.

Simp was half-trotting, half-walking ahead without regard to Bob. He lingered behind. The dirt road led to a sandy summit, where Simp paused long enough for Bob to catch up. Below, the town's garbage for the day lay disgorged from the trucks in rippling mounds like the waves of some foul surf. The air was thick with the smell of rotted food and musty lawn grass.

"By God, will you look at 'em all," Simp said, whispering

for the first time. He paused only for a moment before creeping down the road in a crouch.

When Bob got to the edge, he saw them. Or at least their shapes, dark blobs zigzagging randomly. They were everywhere. Maybe a hundred. Bathed in the dim white of the moonlight, they pulled boxes and plastic bags from the trash, pieces of meat and fruit, and took them away from the flux of the fresh spill to quieter spots for a private feast. Others frolicked and rolled at the rear of the basin, either full already or waiting their turns. Some chased one another along a large bulldozer's pleated metal tracks and made soft throaty snarls, like overgrown cats, a sound unlike any Bob had ever heard. He could have stayed there, watching, listening. But Simp was already shooting.

Bob followed quickly, clicking on the flashlight and aiming it at the first pair of eyes its beam hit. A skunk. He swiveled the gun away and watched it trundle off into the woods. A sound from the bulldozer attracted his light. On the driver's seat, one fat old coon crouched, dabbing at a carton of broken eggs and licking the goo from its paws. He aimed high and pulled the trigger, blinking at the explosion. The coon disappeared over the side. When Bob found it, its chest was quivering in short, spastic attempts to breathe. He leapt up to the driver's compartment to inspect the seat. It was okay. One of the gauge covers was fractured, but there was no telling from what.

Simp fired, loading one shell after another into his rifle. Bob worried that all the shooting would attract attention.

"How many have you got?" Bob asked.

"Dunno," Simp said. "They keep running away from me. I think I hit some. I just dunno for sure."

"We got to get out of here," Bob said. "I'm going to get two more and we go."

Simp said nothing. One coon he hit scrambled clumsily across the mounds of garbage. Bob clicked on the flashlight and waited for it to stop. Then he pulled the trigger. The coon jumped back against the dirt bank and sank behind the garbage. The sound of the shotgun was immense in the night, echoing in the woods. Bob tiptoed through the garbage and found the coon, still quaking. He picked it up by the tail and heaved it away from the mess. Simp was holding one up by the tail, too.

"Right between the damn eyes," he said. He began stuffing it into a sack. "A couple more and we'll be done."

"No. We have enough. Let's get back to the field."

"Shit, Bob, I'm having myself a time here. Why leave?"

"People can hear us. They'll call the State Police. How would you explain what we're doing." The excitement had passed.

Simp stood with the sack in his hand, grinning. "Who cares what they think. It's no crime, aside from trespassing, maybe."

"Apley would find out."

"I didn't think of that," he said, taking the coon Bob had shot and stuffing it into a sack.

Later they scattered the coons in the rear of the field. They'd each shot two. One of them was still twitching when they dumped the bag. Simp pounded its head with the butt of his rifle until it stopped moving. The coons didn't seem so mysterious now. Even the skunk had known enough to leave the dump. But not the coons. As long as there was garbage to eat, they would have stayed. They were just a bunch of good ol' boys, out on the town and too drunk with a good time to care about the consequences. They could have shot every one of them.

For some reason he couldn't recall later, they both returned to their spots in the field, as if there were a point to maintaining the masquerade. Bob was too tired to figure whether he'd been smart to go along with Simp. He had done it, and that was all there was to it. As the sky lightened, his fatigue grew denser until the whole night seemed like a dream. About four-thirty, Bob decided to head home. He walked slowly through the corn this time, not worried about Simp. The edges of the leaves slashed against his arms. He could just barely see over their tops still, the silky part of the ears just coming out. Amid the field, he felt like he had wandered into some still bay of water, warm and teeming with life beneath the surface. He felt as if something could pull him under and drag him along the stalks. He held this fear in his mind like someone holds a strange fruit in his hand that he didn't dare eat. It was like playing out a dream to the end. Letting its consequences occur.

When he got home his mother was up and fixed him breakfast. She was happy to hear they'd gotten the coons. "I can tell you're overtired," she said.

When he tried to sleep, he couldn't. He lay in bed for five hours, staring at the ceiling. Finally, he got up.

When he got to the farm at noon, he felt like he was enclosed by his own fatigue—a clear, thick jell that made sounds seem muffled and distant. As he parked the car next to Apley's pickup, he heard a faint rattling beneath the front seat. He felt around and found Simp's pint. There were a couple of swallows left, so he put it back before heading in to see Apley.

"So you shot some coons last night," Apley said. He was sitting at the kitchen table, eating a sandwich.

Bob nodded. Somehow it didn't seem like a lie to nod.

"Were they tough to shoot?" Apley asked.

"No, real easy." Bob got himself a glass of water at the sink.

"Easy, huh? Any get away that you saw?"

"Maybe a few. It was tough to tell whether they were all out in the field when Simp started shooting."

"That right? Why don't you have a seat, Bob. We need to talk."

Bob set the glass down without drinking from it and took a seat at the table. It was quiet. Apley was breathing deeply, slow and regular. He was holding his chin up with one hand, his elbow on the table, and with the index finger of his other hand, he was tracing the rim of the plate.

"You know, Bob, Dink Rinaldi heard some shots over at the dump last night. You hear any shots other than your own?"

"No. Maybe Dink heard ours echoing off the hillside. It was quiet enough."

"Maybe. Although Dink was pretty sure he saw the lights of a car heading up to the dump."

"Well, I'm sure there are a lot of coons up there. Someone might have been shooting after garbage day."

"Yeah, I'd say someone probably was," Apley said. "And

until I saw Dink up town this morning, I was trying to
figure out how the hell one of the coons you guys had shot
in the corn field could get a ketchup label stuck to its belly."
Apley sat there, looking Bob right in the eyes.

It was just like falling through ice. Apley knew it all, and
here Bob had been trying to bullshit him. He was going to
explain why he did it, but he really couldn't think where
to start. He was going to try to make Apley understand.
But inside he knew there was no point.

"I don't have any excuses," he said. "It was wrong."

Apley laughed. "Wrong? It was stupid. Half-assed. It
wasn't even close to a good stunt. I would have expected
more out of a boy of Ellie's."

Bob knew what he was saying. And what he wasn't saying.

"Don't worry, though," Apley continued. "I'm not going
to tell anyone. Not your mom. No one. You get one stunt
like that on this farm. Because you're family, as much as I
find it hard to believe. But Simp's done. Through."

"What?"

"Right after you leave, I'm going to tell Simp to pack up
and get out of Neugent's house by tomorrow. I only wish
Neugent could come back."

Bob's throat had gone dry. The water was still on the
counter. It seemed miles away.

"Here's what I want you to do, Ace," Apley said. "Take
the rest of the day off. Then come in at five tomorrow for
Simp until I can find a new barn hand."

Bob stared at the back of his hands, trying to avoid getting any more upset. He didn't want to cry in front of his
boss.

"There's no sense in waiting around here," Apley said. "I don't like what I have to do right now any more than you do. Just forget about the whole thing. I will, if you will." He put his hand on Bob's, clenched it, then patted it before leaving.

The house was quiet. Apley's wife was out. Bob sat in the kitchen alone. He decided he wanted to leave before Apley got over to Neugent's house. As he drove past, he saw Simp's oldest boy whipping a weedy patch of black-eyed Susans with a stick. Simp was nowhere in sight.

The next morning Bob finished laying down the lime just before noon. Milking and cleaning up took him about twice as long as it took Simp. When he got out of the barn, he saw Simp tying a mattress to the roof of his old Chevy. He thought about ducking back into the barn and leaving by the back entrance, but Simp had already caught sight of him and waved him over. He had loaded a wood trailer with boxes and odd pieces of furniture and was trying to hitch it to the back of his car.

"Darn it," he said as Bob approached. "Should of done this first. Will you lend me a hand?"

Bob held the trailer post as Simp guided the metal eyelet over the hitch knob. "I'm sorry about what happened," he said.

"It's not your fault, Bob. That Apley was too smart for me, that's all. Imagine, a goddamn ketchup label. Who woulda thought . . ."

"I feel like it was partly my fault. . . ."

"Bull. I took all the blame for it. Told Apley you didn't

want any part of it but that I bugged you all night until you said yes. And you know what else I told him? I said I was damn proud of what I did. I tried to fix things up for me and my wife so we could leave here on our own terms. My way, that is. I said, 'You're not firing me, Apley. I quit.' How about that?"

"What'd he say?"

"Said, 'Call it what you like.' I figure I stood square with him on this one. But it wouldn't turn the tide for me. Because I got off on the wrong foot with Apley. You can't do that with a man—get off on the wrong foot."

Bob helped Simp with a rope, pulling it tight around the boxes on the trailer. "What will you do now?"

"I'm wide open. Anything's a possibility. I figure I'll look for work in Hartford—in a factory or something as a night watchman."

"No more barn hand work?"

"Not in this state. Too screwy with all this old money. How about you? What are you up to?"

"Just school."

"That's best," he said. "But remember, you could pick this place up if you tried. With his boy gone, you could do it. And then you could sell off these damn cows and turn the place into a chinchilla farm. Take it from me, that's the way to go."

Bob shook Simp's hand and said good-bye. Linda was at the upstairs window yelling at him to get inside and help. Bob walked back to his car and saw Apley sitting on the granite slab back step of his house. There were empty beer cans by his feet.

"He gone yet?" Apley said.

"Just about."

"Good. None too soon." He took another swig. "You look totally whipped. Go home. I'll do the barn for the rest of the weekend." He stood up and stretched, then went into the dark of the house.

Bob listened to the cicada as he opened the car door. He sat with his feet on the pavement until he remembered the whiskey. He considered running it over to Simp, but decided he didn't want to talk to him again. Besides, there was just enough left to put him to sleep.

··*The Pile*··

*T*he pile was bigger than it ever had been. Ted was responsible for the barn and increased the angle of the conveyer every other week to accommodate the twice-a-day barn cleanings. He meant to start spreading during the first thaw early in March when the fields were still frozen. But with his wife, Chase, just home after two months in the hospital, he had more on his mind than manure.

"The smell's okay as long as we don't disturb it," Apley told Bob at the time. "But stick a fork in that and we'll all have to hit the road. Ted's got himself a chore."

Just before April Apley asked Bob if he had ever worked the front loader. "It's easy," he said. "I'll have to show you some time." Bob knew what was in store for him.

Apley let April slip by without mentioning the pile. The fields were too wet to run a tractor through them. But every time Bob passed by the equipment shed, he stared at the blue Ford front loader, its new bucket as shiny as a drugstore ice cream scoop. Apley called him to ask if he'd work the first weekend in May. With warmer weather finally arrived, the pile had to go.

"What you do is keep your back to the wind," Apley said, dipping the bucket on the front loader and gouging another scoop out of the pile. But May Day was calm and there was no wind. Apley swiveled the loader around and shook the scoop out over the spreader, filling it for the first run.

"It's not that hard," Apley said, as if Bob's biggest concern was working the bucket. "Just don't jerk the levers; pull 'em nice and easy." He hopped down from the seat and moved his hands as if working the levers. "Eeee-zeee, like that. You got it?"

Bob tried to be tough about it. "Yeah, easy," he said.

Apley clapped his hands together and held them that way as if to say, "Let's get started." He inhaled deeply and seemed mildly surprised. He nodded slowly, "You know, I've smelled that pile a whole lot worse."

Bob didn't care how bad it could get. It was bad enough already. His nose stung and his eyes watered, and if he thought about it, his stomach felt funny, too.

"Come in when you're ready for lunch," Apley said. "And by the way, you're on double time today."

Bob opened his mouth to say, "Great." But he couldn't get the word out. Apley never paid double time. Not even for clearing stones, one by one, out of his corn field. And when Bob remembered how much he ached after that, he could easily imagine what was in store for him.

• • •

By the time Bob filled the spreader full for the fourth time, his stomach clenched, and he got dry heaves. He jumped off the tractor and stumbled into the barn, empty now except for the cows. His stomach immediately relaxed.

Bob had just pushed the scoop all the way into the fecal heart of darkness. Scraping along the cement foundation on which the conveyer deposited the manure, he'd cut a swath into the pile's inner core, a wet region in which all of its moisture had migrated and aged into a brown-green mass the consistency of lava, seething with small white worms the size of fingernail clippings.

Bob took a drink from the barn hose and tried not to head to the house to quit on the spot. The cows chewed their cuds and slapped their tails over their backs to shoo the flies. They were machines, genetically manufactured for the production of milk. They ate, made milk, shit, went dry, were inseminated artificially, gave birth, and started the cycle over. When they got old or their production dropped, they were prodded up a ramp with an electric stinger into a slaughterhouse truck to become another commodity: dog food. Their names seemed odd: Ram's Head Rona and Ram's Head Rebecca, Ram's Head Sara and Ram's Head Sally, each with her own name plaque above her stall. And in the morning, after feeding on the cool grass of the fields all night, they returned, ready to be of service, each to its own stall. Bob asked Apley once how he trained them, and he said, "It's easy once they learn to read." But the way they did it made Bob think they were smarter than he gave them credit for being. They bumped one another away from a wrong turn, and almost appeared pleased when they were chained into the correct spot. He sometimes thought that they were abused. Other times, he didn't consider their lives to be all that bad. Well-cared-for, well-fed, they had all the creature comforts. Their lives were testimony to the advantages of a beneficent dictatorship, provided you didn't dwell on the consequences of growing unproductive.

Bob shuffled back for one last drink. He could taste the rubber of the hose this time, definitely not a good sign. It meant his sense of smell was returning. He was on his way out the back door when he remembered the lime. It was stacked in fifty-pound bags along the wall for use on the barn floor. If it was good enough for outhouses, maybe a couple of hundred pounds would work on the pile. He didn't think Apley would approve of dropping it raw onto the manure pile, but it was either that or dry heaves for the rest of the day. He suspected no one would notice a few missing. So he pulled four off the top and lugged them one by one over to the farthest section of the trough conveyer— right where it exited the barn. He emptied the bags on the conveyer, using the barn shovel to spread the lime evenly. Then he turned on the conveyer system just long enough to run the lime out over the pile. As he turned the system back off, he saw a plume of white lime dust rising and hoped it wouldn't be visible at the house. This concern passed quickly, however, when he heard coughing from the direction of the front loader. When he knocked a cobweb aside and peered out a window, he saw Chase. She stood by the tractor, covered in a white film, rubbing her eyes.

• • •

When Apley had fired his barn hand Simp the summer before, he had held off hiring a new one. At first Bob had been grateful for the extra work. He had earned enough in September leading into harvest to buy a new 35mm camera and to blow a couple of hundred dollars on developing without touching the money his parents expected him to put into a college fund.

After a while, Bob got tired of working ten hours every Saturday and Sunday. By Monday he was exhausted. And cross-country practice every night after school only made him more tired. His brother Carl had beaten him in several critical races. He'd gotten depressed.

Apley cut him some slack by hiring Amil for odd jobs. Amil free-lanced as a farmhand from place to place as needed. His hand had been caught in a baling machine and had a weird dent down the back of it. "It makes for a funny handshake," he joked when Bob first shook it.

Bob immediately liked Amil. That was part of what kept the guy in work. Everyone liked him. He was strong, quiet, and friendly, yet not so big-headed as to have opinions about how to run your operation. He let things go their own way.

Bob remembered sitting in the barn loft with Amil that past September. They were drinking a beer instead of unloading bags of citrus they'd just brought back to the farm.

"I don't know if I can keep this up much longer," Bob said. "I'm tired of working every weekend. I wish Apley would hire a new barn hand."

"Forget it," Amil said. "Not until Ted comes back."

"When is that? Christmas?"

"He's going to make one more pitch for that boy to stay on the farm," Amil said. "He'll get him back up here soon. Wait and see."

"I thought he was into stock cars," Bob said. "Like he wanted to make a career out of them."

"His only career," Amil said, "is getting high and keeping up with his wife. I've heard about him for years. But have you seen her?"

"Once," Bob said. "She's pretty."

"Pretty? She's a knockout." He held his hands cupped in front of his chest to suggest how big Chase's breasts were. "Her sisters, too. A bunch of pretty preppy girls. Rich as hell, the whole family."

"Somehow I can't imagine her getting into the stock car scene."

Amil shook his head. "No way she goes for those rednecks," he said. "No way."

"What's in it for her, then?"

Amil made like he was playing a guitar. "She's slumming for source material. For songs. She's out to become another Carly Simon. I mean, she loves Ted and all. But the places she goes with him—it's all for singin'."

"How good is she?"

Amil shrugged his shoulders and popped another beer. "I don't know. I guess she can play the guitar and sing. But shit"—he took a quick swig—"so can a million other people."

A week later Amil passed out while driving a tractor into the tool shed. It barged into a support beam and part of the roof fell down. He was okay, just drunk. But he denied he had been drinking and that cost him the job.

When Ted showed up that weekend, Apley persuaded him to stay. To give the farm one more chance. Over the next month, Bob's hours were cut dramatically. But he didn't mind. Ted and Chase set up house in the hired hand's place and immediately began having parties every weekend. Bob hadn't been invited, but he felt Chase would ask him over pretty soon. He couldn't wait. There was something about the way she lived that appealed to Bob. As long as there was money and time enough, there was fun. Whatever fun she felt like having. She bought an Arabian horse and boarded it in one of the bull stalls in an empty wing of the barn. She always talked with Bob when she tended to it. She flirted, she sang, she rode. That was her day. Sometimes she'd throw her arm around Bob's shoulder and pull her body tight against his in a way that made Bob believe sex was even better than he imagined. She seemed to mold herself to his body. There was a smell to her, a good smell, but not perfume, and it stayed with him after she was gone.

"Careful," Ted said once when he saw her giving Bob a hug. "You'll burn that boy out before he's even got going."

"Nonsense," she said. "A boy like this runs on pure heat. I think when my sisters come back on Christmas break, you ought to meet them. What do you say? Would you like that?"

"Sure," Bob said.

"You're blushing," she said. "That's charming. He's retroverted after all."

"He's what?" Ted asked.

"He's a throwback," she said. She stared into Bob's eyes.

It was a look that said she wasn't afraid to know what he was thinking and that she already knew what he was thinking and that it was all right to think that. She touched Bob's chest. "You'd be a little goofy at first," she said softly, out of earshot of Ted. "But you'd work out fine. Real fine."

Bob heard from Amil that the police had found cocaine in her car the afternoon of the accident. She'd been headed into town to see her family, who'd just gotten back from Christmas in Guadaloupe. She had said she'd throw a party at their house to have Bob meet her sisters before they went back to school at Miss Porter's.

Either through family money or out of sympathy because of her condition, no charges were pressed. The fact that a town truck salting the roads had clipped the car might have had something to do with it, too. Amil told Bob that the truck crew were shitfaced when the state cops got there. If Amil had had word of their condition, it wouldn't have been hard for the families to have found out. As it was, nothing happened. Chase stayed in the hospital for two months with head injuries, and no one got a ticket.

"How do you like that shit," Amil said. "Coke all over the car, town crew unable to stand, and everyone goes off with no charges. I can't believe all that. What I wonder is where the hell she got the stuff. I've been looking and can't find it."

Chase was still coughing when Bob got out back. He thought about leading her right over to the house, but didn't feel like explaining how she'd gotten covered with lime. So he brought her into the barn for a quick cleanup.

"Ted?" she said. "Where's Ted?"

"He's in the house, Chase," Bob said. "We're going to wash up and go see Ted." She started to wander, so Bob grabbed her by the hand.

"No, no, no," she said, shaking his hand away. "I want Ted."

"In a minute," Bob said. "We'll see Ted in a minute."

Trudy had dressed Chase in dungarees and a sweatshirt. The doctors said she had the mind of a four-year-old. No one knew if she'd recover. Certainly she'd never have her looks back. Her jaw had been shattered in the accident. It gave her head a lopsided appearance—sharp and well defined at the top, indistinct at the bottom, with the chin little more than a flap of puffy flesh.

Bob led her to the barn hose. Before turning it on, he slapped at her clothes softly to knock off as much of the lime dust as possible. She giggled like a baby when Bob did this, squirming as if she were being tickled. The dust was in her hair, too. He ran the water to wet his hand, stroking her hair with it to blot up the film of dust. After the accident, her hair had gone from a smooth blond to brown with a streak of gray on top. It had become coarse. The doctors said that the medication probably brought on the change, but no one knew for sure. Wet, her hair had a sweet smell, he guessed from all the conditioners Trudy said she used to try to bring back the oils. The water of the hose splattered on the cement floor. Then he heard Trudy.

"Chase, where are you?" Trudy shouted. "Chase, come back to the house."

Bob saw Trudy heading toward the barn. She'd be there in a minute. He thought about calling to her, but decided to hold off until he cleaned up Chase. When he turned around, she was hosing herself down like she was in a shower, her shirt thrown to the side. Her breasts were there, in front of him, smaller than he had imagined.

"Chase, what are you doing?" he whispered.

She grinned, holding the hose over her head and letting the water run all over her. She made no attempt to cover her breasts. They were white, the nipples large and erect in the cold water. He didn't know what to do. He thought about getting help. But when he looked at Chase, he couldn't move. It felt like minutes passed. He stepped quickly to the faucet and turned off the water.

Chase stared and blinked at the hose. Bob picked up her sweatshirt and moved closer to her. She looked at him and grinned. He had to get her top back on, and fast.

"Chase . . ." Trudy called. "Where did you go, sweetie?"

Bob grabbed Chase by the shoulders and spun her around. That way, he wouldn't have to look at her breasts. He took her sweatshirt and pulled it over her head, her wet hair smearing up against his face. He could smell the conditioner again, stronger than ever. He struggled to get one of her arms through the sleeve when her arm popped free of his grip and his hand landed on her breast. She immediately leaned back into him, the water seeping into his shirt and pants. He let his hand stay on her breast for a moment, longer than it had to, then he finished pulling down her sweatshirt.

"What is it, Mom?" Ted shouted from the house. "Where is she?"

"I don't know. She got out."

"Trudy, Ted, she's in here," Bob yelled, moving to turn on the water again. He sprayed her with it, from head to foot, and she giggled. He handed her the hose just as the side door to the barn flew open. Ted ran in.

"Chase, what are you doing?"

"I found her in here with the hose," Bob said, turning off the water.

"How'd she get here?" Ted asked.

"It's my fault," Trudy said, coming in from behind. "I was on the phone and thought she was asleep. It was time for her nap. When I checked her room, she was gone."

"She's all right," Ted said, hugging her drenched body.

"Ted," she said softly. It was the voice of love.

"What's going on here," Apley said, rubbing his eyes. He'd been inside for his afternoon nap.

"This poor soul went wandering," Trudy said. "Bob found her in here, giving herself a shower with the barn hose."

"Oh, yeah," Apley said, looking around. His stare fixed on the empty lime bags. "You leave those in here, Ted?"

Ted walked over to the conveyer and looked around. "Not me. Did you, Bob?"

Bob nodded. "I used them on the pile," he said. "I couldn't take the smell. That's when I found Chase."

"I don't blame you," Ted said. "That pile was a beast."

"Oh, come off it," Apley said. "What's a little crap. Really, Bob, liming the manure. You ought to be ashamed."

Apley didn't sound angry. Not as angry as Bob had heard him at other times. But Bob felt ashamed. He knew he looked it. "Yeah," he said. "I'm sick about it."

"Let's not exaggerate," Apley said, slapping him on the back as if it were okay to be weak. "It'll wind up on the fields anyway."

Bob was on top of the ridge spreading the sixth load when he noticed he couldn't smell the stink anymore. He knew it was there. He could almost feel it in the air. Yet somehow his sense of smell had shut down. He wasn't sure whether it was a case of his nose protecting itself, or of his mind blanking it out. Maybe some combination of both. Some merciful act of mind and body to do away with pain or great unpleasantness. He considered that a small miracle. Nothing that would warrant erecting a shrine, but something to respect. As the blades of the spreader slashed through the slop, spraying it in a great semicircle behind him, he allowed himself to feel nothing but the vibrations of the tractor's steering wheel. He shut his eyes for a moment, he didn't know for how long. When he opened them he had almost taken the tractor into a ravine. But the tractor turned easily, and he aimed it toward the gate, confident now that this last pass would cover almost all of the field, and that there would soon be good hay to cut. And that all that remained beyond this was simply to do the job again.

·· *On the Roof* ··

*C*hase's yellow Fiat was towed back to the farm and put behind the barn. It stayed hidden for a while, but after the snow melted, it remained. Bob couldn't understand why they wanted to be reminded of the accident. Once in a while, he would try to imagine how she managed to survive. The snowplow that sideswiped the car ripped off the left side of the windshield and the roof above it, cracked the steering wheel in half, shredded the top of the driver's seat, and tore out the door frame. The popped-out metal looked like a party noisemaker after it's been yanked. It was beginning to rust.

Apley impressed Bob by how well he kept himself under wraps. His joking had turned a little flat, but overall he appeared to be in the same easygoing mood, quick to cut Bob up whenever he did anything wrong. The only other change was in the quantity of beer he consumed. Before the accident, Bob took the fifty-gallon drum filled with cans to the dump about once a month. Now it was close to every two weeks.

Ted wasn't as easy to read. But Bob didn't scc that much of him. He almost always worked out in the fields or was off doing chores when Bob worked. When he was in high school, Ted had been a legendary drinker. Everyone in the family had him pegged to follow in Apley's shoes and to take over the farm. But when Ted grew his hair out and started hanging around with the set of rich kids in town, he changed. Bob had heard people say he grew pot on the farm. But it was hard to imagine Apley not knowing that. When he started going out with Chase, it seemed like he became a different person. And when they took a summer off to hitchhike around the country, the family started talking about Ted as a problem. He got married somewhere out West without even telling anyone beforehand. By the time he announced that he was joining a stock car team as a mechanic, the family had given up on him.

That had been four years ago. When he returned to the farm with Chase the fall before, everyone just forgot his past. His pony tail was gone. He had gotten a little soft around the middle, and his arms were pillowy like a fat man's. But he was still strong. He could carry two cinder blocks pinched together in each hand like they were lunch boxes. The accident had to be bothering him, but you'd never know it from his face. It was like Trudy's—puffy and round—but without animation, an affect that Bob took for either controlled grief or some sort of numbing high.

Trudy was more visibly upset. With Ted home, Bob

wasn't invited in for lunch. There was too much family business to discuss. But he'd catch a glimpse of her once in a while when she came out to fetch Ted or Apley. Her face was whiter, her forehead tight and wrinkled.

Bob guessed that baby-sitting an adult could do that to anyone. What made it worse was the feeling everyone shared that Chase somehow knew, or at least felt, what she used to be, that she had some hazy recollection of former abilities. Once when Bob helped him pile bags of citrus in the barn loft, Apley said he couldn't help feeling that she had just enough of a mind left to know some of it was missing. The thought had never occurred to Bob. He stood there, the tang of citrus dust on his tongue, trying to imagine how awful that would be. Whenever Bob drank orange juice, he remembered what Apley had said.

As far as Bob was concerned, Ted had scored a big coup in marrying Chase. She was rich and looked it. Her face was small and angular, with a thin, perfectly defined nose—the result of two centuries' worth of the eugenics known as good marriages. She smiled easily and often, and used her smile to communicate a range of feelings—from surprise to cool dismissal. That too was a product of breeding. But her face had lost its tone. Her jaw had been broken, and either the doctors hadn't put it together right, or her whole face had dropped.

The second week in August the roof over Chase's room sprang a leak during an all-night thunderstorm. She didn't say a word about it. She beat a path between her bed and the bathroom, bringing towels to sop up the water. When she used up all the towels, she emptied her dresser of sweaters and jeans, and then her closet of dresses, skirts, and blouses. Everything got stained. The water seeped down through the floor and ruined the ceiling in the family room. Trudy was still crying when Bob got to the farm the next morning.

Apley asked Bob to come with him to check the corn. They took the pickup and Apley asked Bob to drive. When they got out on the dirt road, he started rambling.

There was no logic to it, Apley said. The accident, the problems, they just couldn't be understood. Trudy was on thin ice herself. He'd never seen her so upset and nothing seemed to help. She had her heart set on Ted staying, but after this? Who could blame him for leaving? She spent half the day resenting Chase and the other half feeling guilty about it. One thing for sure, she couldn't take looking after Chase for much longer. It was a situation where every other option you thought of just stank.

When Bob swung the truck into the corn field, Apley stopped talking. Bob could feel his stare, and didn't return it. Why was Apley telling him this? What could he do? He started thinking it was high time for Apley and his family to have a little bad luck in life. It isn't all hard work and brains, he found himself thinking. People get screwed for no good reason. Maybe Apley could understand what Bob's father felt like now. Then he felt bad. How could he wish all this on anyone? Especially on someone who'd been so fair with him.

"Do you want me to park here at the edge of the field?" Bob asked finally.

"Oh, well," Apley said. "Got to keep our chin up." He

stared straight ahead into the corn. Bob put the pickup in "park," and opened the door to get out. But Apley shook his head. "Turn back," he said, "the corn's okay."

As they drove back to the farm, Apley said he'd be needing as much help as Bob could give over the last three weeks before school started—from five in the morning to seven at night, if Bob was up to it. There'd be time and a half for every hour over forty. It was perfect. Bob had counted on earning a couple of grand over the summer for college, and maybe enough for a junker of a car. For the first time, it looked like he had a chance.

"We'll start by fixing the roof," Apley said. "You and Ted can tackle that. We'll be doing the whole thing, not just where it leaked. Right down to the beams—so Trudy can relax."

Ted knew about roofs. He also knew better than to get involved stripping the old shingles and ripping out the rotted slats. It was dirty, hot work. "I'll help you set up the tarpaulin and lay down the plywood when you get to it," he said. "We'll work together putting down flashing and shingles, too."

The roof was a bitch. You had to watch what you were doing all the time. Each day, for the first few minutes, Bob felt he was going to fall. That was okay, because he knew he'd be careful. It was later on that things got really scary. When he was sure he wasn't going to fall, when he was nonchalantly tossing old shingles over the edge—that was when he found himself almost going over. He'd get cocky and forget to stay on the board supported by angle irons.

Next thing he knew, he was sliding down the worn surface of the old shingles, following the force of his toss and propelled by his own bulk. There was always a moment—how long it seemed—a split second in which he believed he was going over. After it happened a third time, Bob began to appreciate that moment—that instant of panic. It was more intense than the feel of winning a race, more than feeling like a total fool at a junior high dance. For a split second he truly believed, right down in his gut, that it was all over—he was going down—that all he could do now was to concentrate on falling feet first so only his legs would break. Of course he always managed to gouge and claw to a stop.

The job stretched on for two weeks. Several of the beams below the slats had to be reinforced, and since the house was two hundred years old, Apley fussed over how that was to be done. Everything had to be authentic.

Once a day, Ted showed up at the top of the ladder to monitor Bob's progress. Sometimes he'd head back down without saying a word. When Chase caught sight of him, she would come out from the house and stand on the lawn below, watching. If Ted didn't pay some attention to her, she'd start to act up. "I'm running away," she said once. And she turned and started walking toward the fields in the exaggerated way kids do. Ted let her go until she was out of sight. After a few minutes, Bob could hear her screaming from somewhere near the corn field. Ted didn't say a word. He climbed down and went after her.

Bob's mother had heard from other nurses at the hospital

that Chase had the mental age of a four-year-old. "Sad," she said. "Such a talented girl." The entire family had a chorus of comments to the same effect. Chase was a topic for all of the aunts and uncles and cousins. She was different. Who ever heard of a dairy farmer's wife named "Chase"?

Not in Connecticut, anyway. But it wasn't just the name. And it wasn't the fact that she had been to Miss Porter's School, which she had been enrolled in since the day she was born, or that she had spent two years at Vassar. It wasn't even the fact that she had played guitar and had sung folk songs and had done a demo tape. It was the way she walked that told you she was no farmer's wife. She was too light on her feet, not like a young girl, but as if she weren't subject to the force of gravity. A real farmer's wife walked more flat-footed than that. Jackie, Carol, and Becky had it down. So did Trudy. They walked as if they were prepared to withstand a sudden gust or the blindside whack of a barn door. Chase didn't have to. No barn door would ever have hit her.

She had had it all, and now she had nothing. Bob imagined the drone of Walter Cronkite. "People said she was a girl that had it all . . . and then, the impossible happened." While you're safe in your living room, Mr. Jones, recovering from your rotten little day, the world for someone else is going up in smoke and fire, collapsing in an earthquake, being buried in mud and water or baked to a barren cinder. There were countless catastrophes, coups and assassinations, serial killings, cult murders, mysterious illnesses, carcinogenic chemical dumps. But if you've got your health and a weekly lottery ticket, by God, you've got just about everything a person could ask for in this life. Sure, there are those occasional headaches or bouts of constipation or acid indigestion, but our sponsors take care of those. And that's the way it is . . . this night, tomorrow night, night after night.

Firsthand, though, Bob could see that a catastrophe doesn't make you any more thankful for your life. Instead, it becomes a logistical problem. The shock wears off quickly and in the wake practical considerations take over—those things that must be encountered and dealt with every day on the same level as bodily functions. They weren't even worth discussing.

Ted climbed the ladder carrying two sixty-pound packages of standard black shingles, one over each shoulder. He'd already brought up four packages, and was trying to flip the fifth off his shoulder. But it had slipped too far back during his climb. He held it like a knapsack over his shoulder, his face turning bright red as he strained to pull it up. As Bob slid along the board to offer a hand, he saw the ladder wobble. Quietly, as in a dream, it swayed back from the roof. Ted made a sound with his mouth—not a shout—a sort of gasp, something that might come from a person turning over in his sleep. He let go of the shingles. The ladder hovered in the air like a giant pair of stilts, and Bob shimmied to the edge and held out a hammer. Ted snatched it by the handle, and Bob, holding the claw, pulled. He closed his eyes and shut off his hearing and could feel only the hot stretching of his muscles as he tried to move the ladder and Ted back to the roof. Then Ted flipped the other package to the roof in one great slap, and the aluminum ladder clanked back to the edge.

There was a quiet. A deafness. Slowly, other sounds returned: the hiss of leaves across the street, a car on the road a few hundred feet away, a radio inside the house. Bob looked at Ted, who grinned and said, "Shit."

That was when Bob first noticed Ted had grown a moustache—wispy and long, the whiskers hanging down over his lower lip. "When did you grow that?" Bob asked after Ted pulled himself onto the roof. His hands were shaking.

"Two weeks ago," he said. "I can tell you're pretty observant." He grinned. "I'm going down to get those shingles. Be back in a few minutes."

Ted had been gone for a few minutes before Bob looked over the edge and saw the shingles still spread across the lawn like a scattered deck of cards. Ted was nowhere in sight. Bob thought about getting back to work but decided he needed a break. He lay back on the roof and waited, trying not to think about how close the farm had come to another accident. Then he peered at the ground again. It looked even further down than usual.

Bob lay back down on the roof, its warmth rising into his back, his feet propped against the board. The sky was filled with dark little clouds, the color of bread mold. He couldn't decide whether a storm was coming or had broken up. Someone banged on the ladder to test its position. "Coming up," Ted said. Bob listened to the tap of his shoes against the metal rungs.

"Sorry I took so long," he said, crawling onto the roof. "Had to change my underwear." He grinned and held out a joint. "Thought we could make things up here real safe. What do you say?"

"Why not. Heck, we can't come any closer to falling. You gave me a scare."

"You? What do you think I felt like?"

Bob exhaled. "That would have been a heck of a fall." He handed the joint to Ted.

"Yeah," he said. "That would have been a great fall."

"Have you ever come that close before?"

"Here? No, not here. But when I worked on the stock car crew, I took our car out for a spin after some engine work. I was heading into a corner at about a hundred when the stabilizer bar snapped and I spun out. Bounced off the wall and skidded back into the infield. I think if I'd come off the wall rolling it would have been all over."

The pot was mild. Just right for a roof. Bob watched the smoke cloud he exhaled tumble off toward the horse farm up the road.

"I don't think I'd take either way if it was up to me," Bob said.

"Either way for what?"

"To die. Falling or a car crash." He regretted saying that as soon as the words left his mouth. The pot made him thoughtless.

"You mean if we could choose?" Ted asked, and toked. Exhaling: "Sure, no one would take an auto accident. That's not even in the scope of this discussion. In an accident, you're out of control. We're talking about choosing. You could drive your car over a cliff or something."

Bob found it odd to talk about death so casually. He

enjoyed it. "Nothing in a car," he said. "Nothing off a ladder."

Ted took the stub of the joint and pulled a roach clip from his pocket. "I can't say I'm opposed to the idea of falling. If it was that or cancer, I'd take a fall. Not off a ladder, though. Off a plane. And at least a mile up. Time enough so you could take in the view on the way down. Imagine how free you'd be those last few seconds. You'd have no future to consider, just the moment you were in."

Bob nodded. He hadn't thought about falling in that way. He wasn't sure "free" was the word he'd use to describe it, but the general idea was there. "I'm beginning to think there ought to be more options for us when it comes to death. Nice options. Like a fantasy park. You choose the fantasy, say, a rock-and-roll star or G.I. Joe—you name it—and you do it along with the drug that puts you out. An arcade for death. Think how much Medicare this nation would save."

Ted blew smoke in his face.

"I'm serious," Bob said. "The problem with our prospects is they're all horrible, and death shouldn't be that way. You get cancer or some other disease. You forget who you are and cause pain to everyone you care about. You go in the nuclear flash, or die of the runs from radiation poisoning. Or you kill someone and get the chair. It all stinks."

"In California, it's gas," Ted replied. "They drop a pellet in water, and presto, you're gone. That can't be so bad."

"Bull. You can probably hear the hiss of the gas leaving the water. And when it hits, it probably scorches your nose and fills your lungs with blood and water. I'll bet you feel your tongue foaming and your body twitching before you check out."

"There are other ways. In Texas, it's a needle. What about that? I've got friends in Florida who keep a lethal dose of heroin on hand just in case of a war. They're going to put the Grateful Dead on and check out on one big numbing wave."

Bob whacked the roof with his hand. "There you go. No pain, just pleasure—that's more what interests me." Bob looked over at the barn. He could hear Apley steaming the milking equipment. It would be time to do the herd pretty soon. "Pleasure has the most appeal," he said. "Get a pellet planted in your brain that explodes during orgasm. You come, and boom—you're out."

Ted laughed. "Some women will tell you that's already the case."

Bob was careful when it came to talking about sex. He could talk about death because no one listening could contradict him. But sex was different. Lots of guys had been laid by his age. "Right now, I'd take it any way I could get it," Bob said. "One shot or more."

"No luck with the women this summer?" Ted asked.

Bob could have lied. He could have said he just hadn't had it in a while. But he decided to be truthful. "Not just this summer," he said.

"You're kidding."

"I don't want to sound like I'm making excuses," Bob said, "but, shit, I can't keep up with these guys who spend all summer on the beach or at some house in Maine. Christ, those guys got it made. But by the time I get back to school from a summer of dirty work, my face is pocked with zits."

"You've got a girlfriend, though—right?"

"Yeah, but she's off at her parents' summer house on the Sound. I've already told you what that means."

"So go down and see her some weekend. My father will let you off. For that, he understands."

"I've been down. It wasn't any fun. Too short of a time. She had two twelve-year-old cousins—twins—to look after. And a house full of relatives at night. It's hard to get my parents' car, too. They work on the weekends. Just having a car would help."

"Go out with someone else."

"You got to be careful. Some of the girls around here, they're out for the long haul. They're too serious about it. Their pants come down only for marriage. They're pro-creators. I'm looking for recreators."

Ted lay back on the roof and exhaled, long and slow. "Man, if you knew what I know now. Don't let it bother you. Forget it. I wish I could see women only as procreators or recreators. My problem is . . . what is it, anyway? Everyone needs a good time here and there. But eventually, you expect more in a relationship."

"That's where your procreator comes in."

"No way. Not like you have it figured. Not with the Sears living room and the new pickup. There's a whole lot more."

"Like what?"

"Like a whole lot more," Ted said, shutting his eyes and leaning back on the roof.

Bob wasn't sure whether Ted expected a response. He couldn't imagine what to say. So he sat there. It seemed like minutes. But that might have been the pot.

Finally Ted opened his eyes. He sat up and stretched. "Is it milking time?"

"I don't have a watch. But I hear your dad."

"So do I," he said, lying back down. "I hear him all the time. No matter where I am. 'Keep your chin up.' That's one I always hear."

Bob shut his eyes and drifted. He was a lizard in the sun, somewhere in another land without trees or ponds or snow. Without seasons. A land of baked dirt and hot boulders.

"What would you think about taking that old Fiat if I fixed it up for you?" Ted asked.

Bob opened his eyes and the light stung. He looked over at Ted. His eyes were shut. "Are you serious?"

"Were you thinking of something else? Another car? This won't race a Camaro, you know."

"Do you want to do that?"

"I want to get rid of that car."

"How much?"

"Just what I put into it. Is it a deal?"

"Yeah, it's a great deal."

"It's a good deal. Not a great one."

Bob was quiet. He heard the slap of the screen door to the dairy, and the sound of Apley moving across the dry grass of the lawn.

"How you doing up there?" Apley said from below. "You still awake?"

Those words. Apley had said the same ones nearly a year before when Bob was in the silo. He wore a pith helmet and two sweatshirts to protect him from the silage blowing in from above. He was raking it level, or trying to, in a great warm storm of falling vegetation. It had sat in wagons overnight, fermenting in the heat of an Indian summer. Sour with smoldering greens and the sweet decay of corn kernels, the air was thick the way he imagined it in the tropics. He was in the tropics. On a Caribbean island. So high, so high. Raking the sugar cane and so high when he couldn't move. It was up to his thighs and he was so high. Stop, he was saying. Stop. And he could hear Apley say, cut the auger, shut it down. Bob swayed in the silage, thinking it was time to free his legs. He was being buried. Then Apley showed up. He put a pill under Bob's nose. Bob jerked his head back and smiled. His eyes cried. "You're too high to be in here," Apley said, burrowing around Bob's legs and pulling him out. Apley went down first. Bob's hands were wet and slipped off the cold rungs. But Apley held him up. When Ted drove in and surprised everyone, Bob was sitting at the picnic table. He had never met Chase, and here he couldn't stand up to say hello. She had beautiful sisters, they said. Now he knew it was true. Ted was pouring a dixie cup of wine for him to drink. And Chase was leaning toward him, smiling the way Bob had always hoped a woman would smile at him.

··*Bats*··

*N*ear the end of October the skies became overcast and the air muggy. Apley said the weather was perfect for one last outdoor job: removing the house shutters so they could be painted over the winter. Bob started on the job after school. It was slow work, moving from one window to the next. After each shutter, he got down from the ladder and then lugged it to the next shutter.

The latches of the shutters were painted solid; Bob had to pry them off the side of the house with the claw of his hammer. Each time he popped a shutter forward, he found bats attached to the clapboards. At first, he paid no attention to them. But after a while, bored with the work and curious about the bats, he began hitting them with the hammer. It became a little game to pass the time. How many could he whack without missing? Unless he nailed

them squarely, they made a little squeal, barely audible, as
they fell to the ground, crippled and twitching.

"You better watch out for those little things."

Gruber the junk man was at the foot of the ladder, watching him. Bob hadn't heard Gruber's truck.

"They're all over the house," Bob said.

"They're tough to get rid of once they get in."

"Am I supposed to help you load some junk?" Bob asked.
Apley and Ted were picking up a load of lime. No one had
mentioned Gruber was coming over.

"Naw," Gruber said. "Here to see Trudy."

Gruber was visiting Trudy a lot. He was a minister of the
Church of the Shining Beyond. She attended Saturday ser-
vices he held in an old truck trailer next to his bungalow
by the junkyard. It wasn't really a bungalow, more of an
'old chicken house he had bought cheap and fixed up. The
trailer had old oak movie seats in it. There were probably
thirty members of the congregation.

Bob popped another shutter forward and a bat dropped
down, fluttering off toward the barn. He still wanted a
break, but didn't feel like taking one in front of Gruber,
even if the guy was a jerk.

"I'd say from the look of it you ought to call the exterminator," Gruber said. "Yes sirree, it's time." He jumped
back when the bat fell, and a long slick of hair he kept
combed over his bald spot plopped over his face. He flicked
it back in place as easily as if he were straightening a rug.

"Do you want me to fetch Trudy for you?" Bob asked.

"That's okay," Gruber said. "I know my way around."

Bob climbed down with two more shutters and slid the

ladder to the next window. He had pried off another shutter when he saw the faint image of a face staring at him from inside. He lurched back, startled. Then he saw it was Chase. He smiled at her and said hello, but she didn't respond. She backed into the room until all that Bob could see was the reflection of bare-branched maples in back of him along the road.

He thought about the bats. On the house's south side, there were only one or two behind each shutter. They hung from the lower edge of the clapboards, each about the size of a field mouse, clamped onto the heaves of cracked paint. Roused by the creak of rusty hinges and the glare of daylight, they flexed the thin, webbed flesh of their wings in an effort to fly. He didn't miss those. But as he worked around the house, he found more behind each shutter, until, on the north side, there were close to ten hanging there each time he popped the shutter out.

By the time Bob had worked halfway across the north side of Apley's house he began to feel like he was in a real contest. Nailing one or two bats was easy, but ten or twelve—now that involved some skill with the hammer. At first he was slow and a couple got away. Some even bobbed in the air around him. He slapped one with his hand and it bounced off the side of the house before falling. He supposed it would be unfair to count that as a hit.

After a couple more shutters, he got faster. Whop-whop-whop. Whop-whop. Whop-whop. Whop. Maybe one got away. Then the junk man showed up. He did a few more shutters for form, but grew sloppy. His batting average was down to just a little better than .500, 56 for 110. Gruber had thrown off his rhythm. If the guy had gone in to see Trudy and kept out of Bob's business, things would have been better.

Bob was carrying down two more shutters when Trudy called from the porch. He couldn't see her. "Bob, come down for a second, will you?" she said again. Bob heard Gruber's truck revving in the backyard. It sputtered by as Bob climbed off the bottom rung, its bed loaded with old refrigerators.

Trudy had a pitcher of iced tea, already down a couple of glasses. "The minister tells me you've been finding bats behind the shutters," she said. "He says you shouldn't be hitting them with the hammer because they get mean."

Bob poured himself a glass and took a seat in a wicker chair. "They don't seem mean. I hope I wasn't disturbing you with the banging."

"I thought it was related to getting the shutters off. It's been a long time. . . ."

"Does it bother Chase?" Bob had learned to be careful when working around Chase. Her moods had been completely unpredictable since the accident.

Trudy stared past Bob as if she didn't hear the question. Sliding her wedding band up and down her finger, she opened her mouth, as if she were starting to say something, but managed only to nod her head quickly. She sipped from her tea. "No," she said when she swallowed. "She's not bothered by much, poor soul. Not since we've been giving her the sedatives. Why, she sits in that room all day. But the minister doesn't think that's right. He says we shouldn't be giving her drugs. That she is winding down on her own and pretty soon will be in a state of pure receptivity."

"For what?"

"For the blessed communion, Bob. That's what I'm talking about."

Bob finished his iced tea and thanked Trudy. "I'd like to get back to work now," he said. "I'm sure Apley and Ted would like some help unloading the truck when they get back."

"Those bats, though," she said. "Don't keep hitting them. The minister thinks we'll have to call an exterminator. The tip of the iceberg, he said."

"The bats?"

"Behind the shutters and in the rafters, under the eaves and in the cavities," she said. "That's what he told me."

"I'll show Apley when he gets back."

"There's a member of the church who exterminates."

"Good, give Apley his name." Bob thanked her again and climbed up the ladder. The religious stuff was too much for him to handle. The Church of the Shining Beyond—it sounded like a game show. According to them, life was a series of circles of energy, with the lowest one being the holiest.

Bob's mother couldn't believe Trudy fell for it. "She was such a down-to-earth girl," Ellie said. "You should have seen her take care of Cousin Minnie when she was delirious. She was a trooper."

By the time Ted and Apley got back, Bob had all the shutters down and stacked in the barn workshop. The sky was darkening and looked like rain.

"Got enough lime here to sweeten every acre on the

farm," Ted said as he climbed out of the cab. "I'll be spreading it from now till Thanksgiving."

As they unloaded the truck, piling the bags near the spreader, Bob told them about the bats. And after he thought it over, about what Gruber had said.

"Gruber was here?" Ted said. "Why?"

"I think he looked in on Chase," Bob said.

"Chase?" he said. "What business of his is it?"

Apley slapped lime dust from his shirt and pants. Ted and Bob took turns slapping each other's back. Plumes of white lime hung still in the air, stinging Bob's eyes and coating his tongue with a sticky film. Apley's hair was white.

"We're practically made up for Halloween," Bob said. "Papa ghost, son ghost, and cousin ghost."

Ted pinched one side of his nose and blew the other out onto the ground. "Thought you were going to say the holy ghost."

"I'll leave that to the junk man," Bob said. It was one of those remarks he immediately regretted.

"We don't need to discuss Mr. Gruber," Apley said.

They sat at the picnic table. Ted brought three beers from inside. "Let's wash down that lime dust," he said.

"Odd how something so good for the plants tastes so crummy in the mouth," Bob said.

Apley raised his eyebrows and smiled. It was a simple little expression—but Bob suddenly knew that he hadn't seen Apley smile in a long time.

"I suppose we ought to find something philosophical in that remark," Apley said. "Yin-yang, is it?"

Ted laughed with a mouthful of beer until it was dripping from his nose. "Forget the eastern stuff, Dad. It's not your style."

They drank their beers without talking after that. It was close to dusk and Bob could tell Apley wanted to get on with business. He had a distracted look about him. His eyes were wandering and he drummed his fingers on the side of the beer can. He started talking about the bats. How many were there, Apley wanted to know. About five per shutter? He appeared bothered by the number.

"Have you had them before?" Bob asked.

"Oh, they've been on the farm for as long as I can remember," Apley said. "But I don't think we've ever had them on the house."

Bob was pointing to a few spots where he had seen track marks under the eaves when Trudy came out of the house. "We have to do something," she said, wiping her hands on her apron.

"I suppose we should call an exterminator and have him check the attic out. Did you see any other signs of them getting in beneath the eaves?"

Bob shook his head. "I haven't really looked that close, either. I figured most were behind the shutters."

"One more thing," Trudy said. "It's just one more thing this year. We are being tested. Tested!" She sounded on the verge of tears, her voice throaty and about to crack. "When I think how many times I'm in that attic."

"No cause for alarm yet, Trudy," Apley said. "Heck, this happens all over the place from time to time."

" 'No cause for alarm'? With bats in the attic. Those foul little things. They're dirty, dirty things." She shuddered as she said this.

"Maybe I should hit the road," Bob said.

Ted belched and put his arm around Bob's shoulder. "No, stay here. We're in for a little of Mom's new cosmology. Fasten your seat belts."

Apley gave Ted a look that required no words to understand. Ted raised his eyebrows and drank from his beer.

"Why didn't you say something earlier, Bob?" Trudy asked. "You should have told us as soon as you saw one. We could have done something."

Bob looked to Apley, who nodded at him as if to say, "Relax."

"Well, dear," Apley said. "We know about them now. And now we can do something."

"The only reason we know is because the minister thought to mention it. Otherwise we might not know even now."

"Yes, Trudy," Apley said. "The minister did us a favor by calling our attention to them." He turned to Bob. "Why don't you call it a day, after all."

The next day Apley called. Quite a few things would need to be moved out of the attic so that the exterminator could get to the eaves. "Three generations of boxes up there, and twelve hours to move them," he said.

Bob never expected farm work to include lugging boxes from attic to cellar for the family. He'd been at it for a few hours when he overheard Apley and Trudy discussing where to put all the boxes.

"You're not going to put Minnie's linens in that damp cellar," Trudy was saying. "I won't have it."

"What do you want me to do with them? Put them in the barn?"

"I don't care if we have to rent a house. We're not going to risk getting that stuff wet."

Bob stood at the second-floor landing, holding a box marked "Ted's Baby Clothes." He didn't want to barge into the kitchen with Apley and Trudy arguing. His arms ached. So he sat down on the first step and put the box beside him. If anyone came up the stairs, he'd stand and start down. He shut his eyes for a moment, but the creak of the floorboards down the hall made him look up. He saw Chase duck into her room. He kept his eyes fixed on the spot. Her hair hung out into the hallway before Bob could see her face. She was peeking around the corner the way a clown would—with exaggerated caution and leading with the top of her head. He tried to imagine what she saw of the world, what she thought of it now, after the accident. Did anything make sense? Did she remember Ted was her husband? He knew they didn't sleep together anymore—it would be like sleeping with your kid sister—but did they still have sex just for the heck of it? It was the kind of thing he couldn't ask Ted.

"I'll go find out what's taking Bob," Apley said from below. A door swung open and steps approached. Chase disappeared and her door swung shut. Bob lifted the box and continued down the stairs. It was going to be a long day.

The exterminator came on Friday. He had a crew of three. They wore masks and carted bag after bag of white powder into the attic, along with thin-nozzle blowers. Trudy left as soon as they started. Bob helped Apley with the barn and didn't see that much of the exterminators during the day. Ted was off liming the fields. Bob didn't know what was up with Chase.

When the job was done, the head of the crew called Apley and Bob over. "Don't mess with any bats you find twitching on the ground," he said. "They like to bite when they're dying, just like you would. And I'd suggest staying off the house for a week, too. Let that poison dissipate."

Bob watched the three other crew members whacking each other's uniforms, sending up clouds of white dust that drifted in the faint breeze slowly across the street into the hay field. There were tiny brown lumps lying along the base of the house. They looked like they had been lightly powdered with confectionery sugar. Bob saw one bat that looked like it could still fly. He bent over it, then squashed it with his foot. His season was over—57 out of 111. He could look forward to salary arbitration next spring— maybe even free agency.

"You heard the man," Apley said. "Watch out for those little things. No picking them up."

Bob was free to go, but had left his jacket in the barn workshop. Weather-beaten and flaking, the shutters were stacked on end inside, tilted like a row of dominoes about to fall. He didn't see Ted.

"You going?" Ted asked from an old tractor seat that had been rigged up as a stool. On the bench next to him was a bottle of Jack Daniel clenched in a vise.

"Drinking?" Bob asked.

Ted frowned. "You'd make a hell of a detective, buddy.

Actually I'm just performing some experiments on the bottle." He turned the vise tighter. "Hmmm. How much more . . ."

"I didn't know you went into town," Bob said.

"Didn't. Dad keeps two or three hidden out here. Late night chores when he's pissed at Mom—often enough lately."

"What's happening, Ted? People in the family are wondering."

"Are they? People in this family are wondering, too. What's happening? Let's see . . ." He turned the vise tighter until the metal clamps gritted into the bottle. "I can't tell you what's happening with them. But with me . . ." He gave the metal rod one quarter turn and the bottle exploded—glass flying up and out from the vise, the dark smell of bourbon filling the shop. "This is knowledge," he said. "No more than three turns. Do you know the test for validity?"

Bob didn't know if Ted expected a response, but he shook his head anyway.

"If we can find another bottle of Jack Daniel, could you break it in three-and-one-quarter turns? Because if you could, we'd both have valid knowledge."

"I've got to go now," Bob said.

"So do I," he said. But Ted didn't get up from the seat. He used a metal file to herd the glass fragments toward the base of the vise. Something clicked then. Something deep inside. Nothing was right here. Bob backed out of the shop, not turning his back on Ted until he was in the driveway. His heart beat rapidly. He glanced at the second-floor windows, half-expecting to find Chase staring down at him, but she was nowhere in sight. He could hear the blood in his ears, a rhythmic rushing in and receding, the waves of a small lake. It covered the sound of his sneakers on the pavement, and he felt like he had no body, no body that could be hurt or seen, one that could go in the house and watch Chase, find out what was really going on. He could watch when Gruber came to visit. He could see how Apley and Ted made their peace after days such as these. He could see anything there was to tell about good lives gone crazy for no good reason. He could be that force itself, ruining Minnie's linens, opening the gates for the cows to run off, hiding the tractor keys, or emptying the feed bins. He could move from room to room and bring one thing to an end, another to disaster. He knew now that which he had never known himself, that after all this, there would be questions—why, why did this happen?

··*A Rolltop Desk*··

*W*hen Bob got to the farm he couldn't find anyone to tell him what was going on. Apley's car was gone and the Chevy pickup parked next to the front porch of the hired hand's house was partially loaded with boxes. Ted had called the night before and asked Bob if he could come over after school. He had said he needed a hand with some stuff.

Bob took a seat on the granite front step and waited. He hadn't been to the farm much in the past month. But he could see some big move was under way. He guessed it was Ted. A tweedy couple in a horse-drawn carriage clopped by. The man touched his cap as he passed, the clouds of his breath rotating into the woods. There was a chill setting in. The weatherman said there might be snow on the ground for Thanksgiving. It was just cold enough now to get Bob off the step. His rear felt like it was turning numb. He didn't hear Ted coming around the corner. He glanced at Bob quickly and hopped up onto the truck.

"What's up?" Bob asked.

Ted paused to look at Bob again, and then coughed and spat over the side. He'd had a cold for weeks. Taking a broom out of the posthole toward the front of the bed, he swept the dirt and cow feed from the space which remained. "I need your help loading a rolltop desk onto here," he said finally.

Bob glanced at the boxes and for the first time noticed one stuffed with Chase's sweaters. "Where's she going?" he asked.

"Back to her folks in town."

Last week Bob had seen Ted in town. He had told him that he was thinking of taking a trip with Chase. "A change of scenery," he had said. Her condition had stabilized at the mental age of about six, according to the doctors. The prospect for a full recovery from the accident was remote. But Ted had spoken only of sticking it out with her, and of his new life on the farm.

"You going to watch or help?" Ted asked, jumping off the truck onto the porch. "We got a rolltop desk up there to carry down. That's all. And unloading it, if you don't mind."

"It has me a bit off balance, that's all," Bob said. "The move I mean." Bob guessed Apley wasn't there.

"There's a screwdriver in the glove compartment of the cab," he said. "We need to take the door off."

Ted disappeared into the house while Bob took the door off. He could hear Ted talking on the telephone, but couldn't make out what he said. When he heard Ted's steps on the stairway, Bob headed in and followed.

"Is the thermostat turned down?" Bob asked when he caught up.

"Everything except the power is off," Ted answered. "I just called the phone company." He led Bob down a short hallway. The desk was in a room that was otherwise empty, its door already removed. The desk was at the center of the room. There were footprints surrounding the desk in the floor dust. The house had a dusty smell of being unlived in. The floors cracked with each step. Downstairs, the phone started ringing.

"Shit," Ted said. "I guess they don't shut it off right away, do they?" After hesitating for a second, he ran downstairs to the phone.

Ted didn't come right back. Bob began fiddling with the desk. He tried rolling up the top, but it stuck about a third of the way. He'd seen a big rolltop like this only once before, in the office of the man who owned the factory where his father worked. When the plant was sold, he took the desk with him. Bob peeked inside. Little cubicles catacombed the back panel. He saw some papers sticking out from the upper cubes but couldn't reach them. The top wouldn't budge. When he heard Ted coming back upstairs, he stood up straight.

"The goddamn thing was her grandfather's. You know, I can't remember bringing this thing in here. I mean, I can remember taking it out of storage in Raleigh. And I can remember how hard it was to load on the truck, but I can't remember unloading it. I can't remember bringing it up the stairs. I was either drunk or didn't do it."

"The top doesn't work," Bob said.

"Yeah. It's been stuck for years. Maybe it's time the damn thing got left behind." Ted banged on the top, trying to loosen it. "When I talked with Chase's father the other night about this move, he said, 'You'll be bringing the desk back, I assume.' This is before I've even explained what's going on. And all he wants to know is about this desk."

"Were you close with them?"

Ted laughed. "They aren't even close with one another. They farmed the girls out to prep school before they had their first periods, and sent them to camp all summer. Chase used to joke about it. She said she and her mother had a good correspondence. They're all back for Thanksgiving, though. All of them."

"How many are there?"

"There are three younger sisters, a couple about your age." Ted gave Bob a solemn look. "Forget it, man. You can make up your own mind, but if I were you, I'd find a nice country girl. Don't bother talking to these girls. They might not even let you."

Ted left the room and came back with a sheet. "When I lift up, you slip the sheet under and we'll slide the desk to the stairway."

Ted set the desk back on the sheet and Bob put his shoulder to it. When he pushed, Bob couldn't believe how heavy the desk was. It was like putting your shoulder against a wall.

"How many times have you moved this?" he asked.

Ted winced. "Too many."

When they got the desk to the stairway, Ted positioned himself on the down side. All Bob had to do was keep the desk centered. But its weight was too much. It spun slowly away from Bob's grip at the landing, pinning Ted against the wall and breaking the window.

"Don't worry about it," Ted said as he pushed the desk back. "Dad said he's going to go over the whole house anyway."

The final set of steps was negotiated more easily. From the bottom of the stairway, it was a straight shot to the truck.

Ted exhaled, his face covered with sweat despite the cold. "Look at me. It's the goddamn booze. I feel like I'm dying."

Bob locked up the tailgate. "Is all this going to the house?"

"Out back, probably. They've got a whole apartment that's empty over the garage. Old servants' quarters. Enough room for three loads like this if Chase had that much."

Bob got into the cab without asking the one question he was dying to ask. He wanted to know what had happened over the past week. But Ted didn't appear to be in a mood for explanations. He talked about the boxes and the desk as if they belonged to some distant cousin. He started up the pickup, and before putting it in gear, he motioned toward the back and said, "I suppose we ought to cover that box there. . . ." He pointed to the sweaters. "Don't want the wind blowing that stuff all over the place."

Bob hopped out and put a smaller box on top of the sweaters. He wondered if he'd call his wife's sweaters "stuff" under similar circumstances.

Ted didn't turn to watch Bob get in the cab. He started driving when the door slammed. As they neared town, the houses got larger and whiter: colonial houses with rambling extensions and turquoise-colored downspouts, formal gardens, and large lawns.

"Is Chase already there?" Bob asked, wanting to find some way to break the silence.

Ted nodded. "Last night."

"Was it tough?"

"It is tough." Ted turned and looked at Bob. It was a look of resignation, of restraint. A look that acknowledged there were many questions that could be asked. Bob fiddled with the dashboard knobs for the pickup's heater, trying to get air blowing on his side of the cab. The glass was fogging up.

Ted turned into the driveway of Chase's house and headed to the old stable and apartment in back. The servants' quarters were larger than his parents' ranch house.

"Is Chase going to live here?"

"I don't know what they're going to do with her. Right now, she's in the house. They might end up institutionalizing her if her mood swings get any more dramatic."

A gray-haired woman emerged from a back door. She wore a beige wool sweater and green plaid wool slacks. "Evelyn," Ted said as she neared the cab. "Chase's mother."

Evelyn rubbed her hands and blew into them. "Is this everything, Ted?"

"This is it," he said.

"You'll come in, of course, once you've unloaded. We do need to talk." She turned to Bob, "And you, too . . ."

"Bob."

"Yes, Bob, for a mug of cheer or something. A beer if you

want. I'll send Wes out presently to explain where he wants this load."

"Upstairs like the last one?"

"Oh, who knows with Wes?" said Evelyn. "I'll let him say."

While Evelyn walked back to the house, Bob dropped the tailgate and leaned against the edge of the bed. The man he supposed to be Wes emerged from the house, walking briskly toward the truck. He was tall and thin and wearing a blazer with some kind of emblem over the chest pocket. One arm swung with exaggerated intensity as he walked, while the other was cocked at the elbow as if about to shake someone's hand. It held a pipe.

"What's Wes do?" Bob asked.

"You're looking at it," Ted said, turning away from Wes's sight. "He walks from that door to the stable and back again. He's a lawyer. Maybe settles an estate now and then. Only the blue bloods, though."

"Is this the 'Bob' you told me would help?" Wes said when he got to the pickup. He banged his pipe on the bumper of the truck and peered at the bowl. Then he extended his hand to Bob. "Pleased you could make it. A big help. Especially with Thanksgiving tomorrow. So much to do in the house." He patted Ted on the back. "All the girls are here, Megan at the last second this afternoon when she heard Chase was coming home. All the way from Chicago on standby. An heroic effort."

"I know," Ted said. "You told me this morning."

"Did I?" he said. "So many conversations. The phone ringing all day. It's like . . ." Wes lowered his eyelids and stared at his feet, waving his hand slowly in front of his mouth as if trying to smell the air. It seemed every rich person in Litchfield had some kind of nervous affectation.

"It's chaos," Wes was saying. "That's all. And I know it's tough for you, too."

Ted picked up a box. "Yeah, it is. Where to?"

"The boxes, right." Wes put his free hand at the base of his neck and massaged it as he thought. "Right where the last load went, don't you think?" Wes rotated his head. "Yes, that's the spot." He tapped the bowl of his pipe on his palm.

"Even the clothes?"

"Certainly. Evelyn will go through them and bring in what's needed, I suppose. And there's room up there for Daddy's desk. It's a beauty, isn't it? Chase loved it and that's why he wanted her to have it. Didn't she love that desk?"

Ted nodded. "She loved it." He moved to the doorway of the stable. Bob picked up a box and followed.

"Before you start, Ted, I wanted to show you the walls."

"The walls?"

"The old walls, leading down along the property in back. I've been working on them for three weeks. You should see them."

Ted set the box down by the door. His face appeared tightened again.

"Oh, it'll only take a sec," Wes said. "Look."

Bob and Ted walked around the corner of the stable. A well-mown field sloped down to the brook at the far end of the property. Perfectly level stonewalls marked the boundaries on either side.

"I didn't know anyone around here could do walls like that," Ted said.

"That's something, isn't it?" Wes said. "A bunch of Italians from Waterbury. Worked like demons. Only one of them knew English." Wes paused and looked around.

There was a sound coming from the dry leaves along the wall, a sound like dry sand being shaken in a bag. Suddenly it started to sleet. The little ice crystals looked like sea salt.

"Anyway, I'll get on with it," Wes continued. "Someone over at the club gave me the name of the one who spoke English. He says, 'Cash only. No checks.' Just like that. So I say, 'Sure, cash. And you'll declare it, too, won't you?' I wasn't born yesterday when it comes to this sort of thing. This little Italian looks me right in the eye and says, 'We declare everything.' A cool cucumber, that one. Real calm."

It was sleeting harder now. Bob's hair was covered with the crystals. "This stuff can't be any good for the desk," he said.

"Good thought, Bob," Wes replied. "Yes, let's get on with it. And come in after."

Despite the sleet, Ted and Bob didn't take the rolltop in first. They carried in the boxes of clothes. When they got to the desk, it was wet and slippery. Ted found a cloth to dry it off well enough to grip it.

"So many of these kinds of desks come apart in sections," he said as he rubbed. "But not this one. That would be too easy. There's just no simple way to carry it around."

Sliding it out of the truck, Ted lost his grip and the desk slipped to the driveway, cracking like a tree in a storm. He quickly leapt down and helped Bob lift it off the ground. There were no visible scars. A pebble had been pounded into a back leg, in a spot no one would ever see. Ted popped the pebble out with his shoe. Otherwise, the source of the cracking sound could not be found.

When they got the desk upstairs, Ted slid it against a wall by himself. As he pushed, his hand rested on the rolltop and it opened partway. He pushed harder and there was a pop. The rolltop opened all the way.

"Shit," he said. "Wouldn't you know I'd finally get this thing working when we bring it back here. Probably snapped some joint back into alignment when we dropped it." He looked in the cubbyholes and found the papers Bob had seen earlier. There were some letters and odd pieces of paper. He folded and stuffed them in his shirt pocket. "Let's go in and get this over with. It's late."

Ted tossed the papers in the front seat of his cab before heading into the house. "They're probably going to want to talk to me alone. You understand. There are *arrangements* to be made," he said sarcastically.

The smell of turkey wafted out of the house when Evelyn opened the door. "Oh heavens, it's a mess out. Come in and warm up."

The house was old, with wide floorboards that creaked and door jambs out of alignment. But the kitchen had been recently remodeled. Large new windows gave a view of the stable and part of the field.

"We're doing our turkey tonight to make the morning easier," Evelyn said. "Here, Bob, have yourself a cup of hot punch while Ted joins us in the study. We've got some details to attend to."

Evelyn scooped a cup of something that looked like spiked cider from a pot on the stove. Bob sat down at a circular oak table by the windows.

"We won't be long," Ted said before leaving.

As Bob sat there, he could hear steps overhead. He wanted to see Chase's sisters. It was getting dark now. Dark enough so Bob could see his own reflection if he looked one way in the window. But if he changed his focus, he could still make out the pickup and the white of the sleet starting to accumulate on the ground.

He flipped back and forth as he drank his punch, staring at his reflection for a while, and then at the pickup until he heard steps coming down the back stairs. Two girls about Bob's age came laughing into the kitchen. Both wore dungarees torn at the knees. One had a loose turtleneck jersey on, the other, the blonder of the two, a Williston sweatshirt.

"I'm Morgan," the one with the sweatshirt announced. "This is Tyler."

"And you're the boy who helped Ted?" Tyler asked.

"Bob," he said, standing. They bumped into each other.

"That was nice," Morgan said. "Thank you."

Tyler hit Morgan's arm with the refrigerator door as she opened it.

"Will you watch it," Morgan said. "Jeez."

Tyler bent over to open a cupboard door, her turtleneck sliding up and exposing the lower part of her back. She stood up with two cups. "Let's try the punch," she said. "How is it, Bob?"

"Delicious," he said, feeling the alcohol warm his insides.

"Will Mom be mad?" Morgan asked. She took a cup from Tyler. "Oh, what the heck."

"How's Chase?" Bob asked.

Tyler tilted her head when she looked at Bob. She made
a soft smacking sound with her lips and glanced at Morgan
before answering. "She's asleep finally. Sedated. She's better than she was, I guess."

"We didn't get back until this morning," Morgan said.
"Last night appears to have been tough."

Tyler filled both cups with the ladle. Bob could hear the
crack of the study door and the muffled voices of Evelyn
and Ted becoming clearer for a second. Then Wes's voice:
"I'll be right back for a cocktail, Eve, after I see Ted off."

Morgan and Tyler looked at one other. Morgan beck-
oned in the direction of the stairs and the two turned and
darted up them.

"So will they let you go to Jamaica with Rooter or not?"
Tyler asked.

"I don't know," Morgan said. "I haven't asked exactly."

Tyler's giggle was the last thing he heard as a door upstairs shut.

"I consider it a temporary change of venue for you, that's
all," Wes said, his hand on Ted's shoulder as they came into
the kitchen. "There's no need for finalities. Evelyn will
understand. You have yourself a good winter up there and
we'll take good care of Chase. You need some time alone,
that's all."

Bob stood up and set his cup in the sink. Wes opened the
door for them.

"And, God, Bob, I almost forgot." He searched the side
pockets of his blue blazer and then the inside ones. "Here
we go," he said, pulling out a crumpled bill, which he
placed in Bob's hand. It was twenty dollars.

Bob opened his mouth to say he was already being paid,

but Wes shook his hand in Bob's face.

"I insist," Wes said. "And, I'm sure you're the kind of boy who'll declare it." He chuckled at his own joke. "No, seriously, you did a yeoman's job today. You earned it."

When they got back in the truck, Bob asked Ted why he didn't tell Wes he was already being paid.

Ted shrugged his shoulders. "What's the difference? They don't need it." He started up the truck and backed it around quickly. "I'm sorry this went on so long."

"That's okay," Bob said. "The pay's great."

Ted bounced the pickup in reverse out the driveway; the papers from the desk fell off the seat as the truck fishtailed onto the slippery road. Bob picked up the paper that landed by his feet. As he set them back on the seat, he noticed one that was a letter to Chase while she was at Vassar. The return address had Ted's name and the farm's road. Ted didn't try to pick up the papers on his side of the cab, so Bob left them there.

As they drove through town, the streetlights flashed rhythmically above. Ted kept his eyes on the road. A couple of times his breathing shifted, as if he were about to say something. But he didn't. Finally Bob felt like he could ask. After all, he had helped.

"So . . ." Bob watched Ted through the flash of a streetlight. He still stared straight ahead. "You're headed up north?"

Ted swallowed. "Yeah. To a ski lodge. I'll work there for the winter. It's . . ."

Bob waited for Ted to finish. They had passed out of town now and there were no more streetlights. The cabin was dim in the faint glow of the dashboard lights. The sleet stuck everywhere now except for two tire tracks in their lane.

"I woke up Monday and I knew I couldn't stay here. And I couldn't leave Chase with Mom. That would have been too much."

As they turned into the farm's driveway, Bob saw the kitchen lights. Apley's car was back.

"You want to come in for a second?" Ted asked.

Bob opened the door but didn't get out. "Naw," he said. "I've got to be getting home."

"That's best," Ted said, shaking his hand. He opened his door, got out, and turned to Bob. "Especially when you feel that way." He reached back in and scooped up the papers off the seat and the floor on his side. "I'll give you a call before I leave."

Bob walked the three miles home, the sleet grinding beneath his steps. He imagined he was crushing salt, breaking it down, each fractured piece in the exact shape of the larger one just destroyed.

··*Prospects*··

*C*hase was gone. Ted was gone. Now Trudy had taken off with Gruber the junk man. God had called her to the Church of the Shining Beyond. Apley was in a funk, but who could blame him?

Trudy also put an end to farming. She took thirty thousand dollars from the farm's bank account. To get rid of the loan for the new milking parlor, Apley sold half of his Guernseys. He sold the other half the next month to wipe out all other debts on the place. "I'm free and clear," he told Bob.

Bob knew it didn't make sense to keep him working. So he was grateful to have a job for the summer. One that kept him out of the factory where his father had worked for twenty years, and where his brother passed the long summer days of his vacation sweeping floors and counting oily brass clips for an inventory no one asked for. He needed every cent for college in the fall. The scholarship guy at school insisted Bob's parents could afford to come up with a thousand dollars. But they told him there was no way they could do it.

Bob got five dollars an hour to paint the small barn that didn't need painting, to sweep out the big barn without any cows in it, and, at the beginning of August, to start shingling the big barn's roof, even though that had been done just five years before.

The only animals left on the farm were two huge Yorkshire hogs that lived on the sour milk that remained in the walk-in cooler. At the end of each day's work, Bob drove two five-gallon pails of it out to the hogs. There were only two hundred gallons of the bad milk left and Bob supposed Apley would get rid of the hogs when that was gone.

Bob was shingling the roof the first time he saw Stub.

"Hey, where's my uncle Apley?" he shouted at Bob.

Though Bob had never met Stub, he guessed it was him. His shoulder-length hair and the red bandanna wrapped around his head matched the person he had heard described in stories as Apley's "hippie" nephew. Bob had also heard that he was missing the ring finger on his right hand—his older brother had accidentally slammed shut the tailgate of a pickup on it, severing it cleanly.

Bob shrugged at Stub. "In town, I think," he said.

"Do you know if he has any work this summer?" Stub shouted.

"No cows," Bob said. "There's not too much to do."

"Yeah, right," Stub said. "That's why he's got you on the goddamn roof. Nothin' for this side of the family, though." He grinned at Bob to let him know it was nothing personal. Bob climbed down the ladder and introduced himself. He got Stub a glass of ice water. They sat on the granite back step to Apley's house and talked for a few minutes until Apley's pickup rolled into the yard.

"Eugene," Apley said when he got out of the truck, "your dad send you over to spy on me?"

"No way," Stub said. "He doesn't know where I am—ever." Stub laughed at himself. "Naw, I need money, that's all. I was wondering if you had any extra work this summer."

Apley crouched in front of Eugene. "Moooo," he said. His breath smelled of beer. "Now that's as close to a cow as I've got." He stood up and laughed. Stub laughed, too, an ass-kissing kind of laugh, the kind you hear from the sidekick to the host of a late-night talk show.

"I don't mean to be funny," Apley said. "Bob will be doing all I need right now. He was here first, and besides, he's going to college in the fall. You probably don't have plans like that, do you?"

Stub grinned without answering. "I don't have any plans today except to look for work. Maybe to go swimming."

Apley looked at Bob. "That's an idea. It's too hot to shingle anyway. Why don't you and Eugene go swimming."

Before Bob could say anything Stub said, "Sure, come along with me. We'll go up to Mohawk Pond."

Bob figured he could do without one afternoon of work. And a swim sounded like a good idea. He climbed into

Stub's Rambler. As Stub backed it around, he looked at Apley. "Hey," he said. "You hear from Ted lately?"

Apley's face loosened and his eyes fluttered before focusing again on Stub. He walked over to the car and leaned with his hands on the door. "No," Apley said. "But I suppose I will soon enough."

Stub went to a vocational school, so Bob's sole source of information about him was the family gossip that had him figured for no good. A do-nothing just like his father Andy. His blond-haired brother Ronnie was a big local jock in soccer, basketball, and baseball. The University of Maine had given him a baseball scholarship. He made the starting rotation as a freshman.

People in the family claimed Ronnie resembled Apley in too many ways to be just coincidence. Then again, people said when Apley used to deliver the farm's milk around Litchfield, half the babies in town had blond hair. Ronnie and Stub: how could you explain the difference? Stub's mother wasn't saying—she had died of breast cancer when Bob was still a boy. Supposedly it was the only time since the split up of the farm that Andy had stood next to Apley. Andy was a lush. The story was that Apley had to buy him out because things were so bad.

Andy hit all the town's bars several times a week, telling anyone who would listen that Apley hadn't given him a fair price for his share of the farm. It was just more of the same old family stink, Bob thought. A way to kill the time.

On the way to the pond Bob kept staring at Stub's missing finger. It was just a nub, barely protruding from his hand

and whiter than the rest of his flesh. Stub noticed Bob's staring and said, "Sometimes when I trip I think it's growing back." He pulled a joint from his pocket and lit it with the dashboard cigarette lighter.

After a few hits Bob was pretty stoned and said, "This shit is good."

"Grew it myself," Stub said.

"So you are a hippie," Bob said, not knowing what the words meant once they left his mouth.

"A hippie? Shit, no. I'm just a little businessman. An entrepreneur."

"Why do you need a job, then?"

"Cash flow. My latest crop isn't ready for harvesting. I just need a hundred or so bucks to stay messed until the buds are ready. After that, I'll have enough to sell to avoid working until next summer."

Bob nodded. Everything Stub said made sense. He liked the guy. It seemed to Bob that while he toiled away on a roof, Stub had things pretty well figured out. Although Stub might not be what a guidance counselor considered college material, Bob saw in him a savvy for business. Not that the family would be impressed by the way he applied it. But to hell with what the family thought. Stub could do something Bob couldn't. And that gave Bob an uneasy sense that he was working too hard, playing things too straight.

Mohawk Pond was a demilitarized zone. Kids from at least five different towns used it for swimming, but no one got in fights. People shared their beers and joints and were polite. No one wanted the Rangers to start patrolling the place. It was a state park with no public beach and no one was allowed to swim there. It had the best water in the area, spring-fed, cold and clear. And in one spot there were low cliffs at the water's edge. Someone had rigged a thick rope to a big tree up there, and, like Tarzan, you could swing out over the water maybe twenty feet up, and jump.

A path led to the pond. Someone with a dark blue Saab was already there. When they got down to the water, Bob saw two girls swimming. As they pulled themselves over the ledge at the water's edge, he saw their breasts bouncing in exertion. He started to feel he was in the right spot at the right time. He hadn't been to the pond that summer. When the girls got closer, he could see one was much taller and more attractive than the other. Why was it, he wondered, that every good-looking girl he knew hung around with a toad. They climbed back up to the rope and nodded to Stub. The taller of the two, her shoulder-length hair wet and smooth, smiled at Bob. It practically drove him nuts just to look at her. But he nodded as if everything was slightly boring. After she jumped back in Bob turned to Stub.

"You know them?"

Stub nodded.

"The tall one's okay," Bob said.

Stub nodded again. "Yeah. She's pretty. She's got a boyfriend, though. I'm surprised he's not here."

There was a rustling up the path and Bob turned to look. Two guys were coming toward them. Both looked like dirt farmers. One wore an NRA hat and was carrying a case of beer. Stub put his hand with the missing finger on Bob's arm for a moment. The gesture sank Bob's spirits.

"Stubby," the guy with the NRA hat said. "You all fucked up again?"

Bob met the guy's stare head-on, wondering whether they were in for some trouble.

Stub appeared indifferent. "Jeez, Dwayne, I guess not," he said. "Even an addict like me needs a break every now and then."

"Who's your buddy? Another doper?" He refocused his gaze on Bob.

Bob stood up. The pot made his head swim and he knew he couldn't fight. Stub jumped up. "Now do you think I'd hang around with scum like that?" he said. "You almost piss me off enough to kick the shit out of you." He grinned the biggest Cheshire cat grin Bob had ever seen, turning his stare to the other guy. "What about you, Bill?"

Bill laughed. "Who? You, Stub? Spank me if I ever think you're messed up again. C'mon, Dwayne, let's find the girls."

Bill nodded to Bob. "Here," he said, setting the case on the ground. "Take a break from the weed and enjoy a few brews."

"Didn't I tell you they were my friends," Stub said to Bob.

"Some of the best," Dwayne said.

The girls were back up on the rock and any tension was gone. After they all jumped in, Stub tapped Bob on the shoulder.

"Friends of Ronnie," he said. "Farmer-jocks."

Bob stared at the black-haired girl. Dwayne had gone underwater and she screamed as he came up between her legs. "What's she see in him?" he asked.

Stub shrugged. "What's anybody see in someone? What's so great about the human body? It's basically bald, and for the most part clumsy. And, as a ratio of its weight, it's not all that strong."

Bob took a swig from a beer and watched the couples below. Stub stood, wrapped the rope around himself, and ran off the ledge, swinging beyond the foursome. At the farthest point, the rope yanked taut, spinning Stub as it unwound. He dove, twisting into the water. Bob finished the beer and caught the rope as it swung back the second time. He took a running start and, not so imaginative as Stub, let himself drop from the rope. He hit the water feet first, the cold stinging his body. At the lowest point, he opened his eyes and watched the bubbles rise to the surface, the clear sky above shining like another world. College was a month and a half away, and he at least had a job that paid him to get stoned. He broke the water laughing at the thought of Carl working in the hot dust of the factory.

Apley sat on the granite step at the back door when Bob arrived at the farm the next morning. It was only nine and he had a beer in his hand. He noticed Bob staring at it and smiled. "The best cure for a hangover I know of," he said. "So how was your swim?"

"Great," Bob said.

"Well if things stay as hot as they're calling for, I expect you'll be taking a few more swims before the summer's out."

Bob didn't respond. "I can't let it dig too much into my work time."

Apley waved at Bob. "Heck, a boy's got to have some fun, too. Consider it a fringe benefit." He finished his beer and tossed the can toward the back door. "How's Eugene doing?"

"Okay. He's a nice enough guy."

"A little hairy, though. Not like his brother."

"I guess not. But not so different from anyone else."

Apley rubbed his chin with his hand. "I suppose not. Ted looked like that not too long ago. He might look like that now, for all I know."

Bob stooped to lift a package of shingles, but Apley stopped him.

"I want you to come with me to the alfalfa field first," he said. "Something's into it. I think it's going to crap out on us before a second cutting."

When they got there, Apley pulled a handful of alfalfa up and showed it to Bob. There were tiny blotches on the leaves, a blight. "What's it mean?" Bob asked.

Apley gazed off beyond Bob toward the farthest point in the field. "Spraying, I suppose. But I can't tell whether it's worth it. I'd have to get a buck a bale."

"Can you rent the sprayer?"

"Not legally. You're supposed to be certified by the state."

Bob was worried that if he didn't get on the roof soon, the shingles would be too hot, and his boots would gouge scars in their tar. The day would be lost. He was relieved when Apley headed back to the truck.

"So did Stub pump you for information?" Apley asked when he started the pickup.

"Information?"

"About the farm. About what I'm planning to do."

"Naw. He wasn't like that."

"Really? I'm surprised. I thought he was looking for bad news like a fly for shit."

Now, with things on the slide, Apley was no longer the picture of self-confidence. After two years of putting up with Apley's little barbs about his father, Bob was glad to see him get a taste of failure for himself.

"I'll tell you one thing," Apley said as he pulled into the farmyard. "I'll be wearing a dress before I bring my goddamn brother back into this operation. I'll let it go to hell first."

After dropping Bob off, Apley left for town to check out his spraying options. He wanted Bob to stick around for a full day, even if it was too hot to shingle, to keep an eye on things.

Bob lugged three packages of shingles to the roof, pausing to rest after bringing each one up. It was close enough to noon to take a lunch break. He went in through the mud room and paused to look at Ted's overalls. They were caked with shit. Trudy hadn't gotten around to cleaning them before she left. The room had a hot, dusty feel, and the boards creaked so loudly Bob was surprised he had never noticed the sound before.

He pulled a quart of milk from the refrigerator, and the makings for a bologna sandwich. He ate the sandwich in a few bites, and stood up, the milk in hand. He drank directly from the carton and put it back into the refrigerator. He

could see into the dining room. Piles of paper covered the
table. There were boxes stacked in the corners. The sight
of them was too much for Bob to resist.

The funny thing about a small town like Litchfield was
the price people paid for the pretense of privacy when their
lawn men, carpenters, painters, and laborers knew every
seamy detail about them and told everyone else. Not that
Apley was the richest guy in town, but his family had been
there for more than a century and, as far as the ground
rules of old money went, that was long enough. What the
plebs gossiped about was of no lasting consequence to people like Apley, and ultimately only an expression of their
stunted lives.

Bob drifted amidst the mess, his trespassing given license
by the lie he told himself: he wasn't looking at anything
that wasn't in plain view. He did no lifting. He saw
enough—appraisals by real estate agents, tax assessments,
accounts of major capital improvements—and he knew
Apley was about to sell out.

He kept walking from room to room, then up the stairs.
If Apley sold the place, well, it was his to sell. Yet the
thought that Apley might throw in the towel left him with
a tinge of sadness, like what he felt at the end of a holiday
when he faced up to going back to school.

Bob paused before opening the door to the room where
Chase had stayed after the car accident. Listening for Apley
and hearing nothing but the cicadas, he opened the door.
The room was warm and stuffy and sweet, its windows
shut tightly, but the curtains were open, a flood of bright
midday light pouring in. The bed was stripped. The sweet
smell—a perfume Bob thought. He shuddered.

He backed out, facing the room as he retreated, shutting the door as quietly as he had opened it.

Bob glanced into Apley's bedroom. The room was strewn with old work clothes and had a musty smell Bob associated with his bachelor uncle's apartment in New York City. Apley's double bed had no bottom sheet on it. Just one white, wrinkled, and messy cover sheet, and two pillows without cases scrunched up against the headboard as if Apley had been reading.

Bob found himself in Ted's bedroom before he consciously wondered whether he should continue snooping. Most of Ted's clothes still hung in his closet or were stacked on top of his bureau. At the sound of a truck Bob grabbed a water-logged copy of *Trout Fishing in America* and left the room quickly, racing downstairs and into the kitchen. From the kitchen window over the sink he could see it was one of Abbott's trucks—a cherry picker Abbott used in his work as a tree surgeon. Bob's heart thumped wildly, and he decided to get out of the house. There was nothing to do out there. It was too hot for the roof. But at least he wouldn't be tempted to roam about inside.

Bob was sitting at a picnic table reading the book when Stub's Rambler pulled in the driveway. Stub saluted Bob as he came to a stop by the table, the odd gap where his ring finger should have been making his hand look like it had horns. "Let's go swimming," Stub said.

"Gotta feed the pigs," Bob said. "I was waiting for Apley to get back."

"Those fat things? They'll make it a day without milk."

Bob shook his head. "I've got to."

"You don't gotta do anything. If you want to, that's another thing. You want to?"

"I should," Bob said.

"You should?" Stub shook his head slowly. "So be it. Where's your car?"

"My mother's got it today."

"And I suppose you got to use mine to tote the milk if you want to go swimming."

"Unless we want to carry it by hand."

"What's this 'we' shit? It's your chore."

"Hey, if you didn't want to help, why'd you drive over? Looking for smut about Apley?"

Stub grinned. "Nope. I leave that to the old man."

Bob set two ten-gallon pails of sour milk on the floor of Stub's Rambler. He hadn't loaded them to the top for fear they would slop over when the car hit the bumps of the dirt road ahead. The tar ended just beyond the hired hand's house, and the road that followed was an obstacle course of potholes and ruts. The pigpen was about six hundred yards up the road. None of the curdled milk spilled, but between the heat and the motion of the car, its thick rancid smell filled the car.

"Jesus," Stub said, waving his hand.

Bob nodded, holding his breath. "Drive," he said on the out breath.

The boar looked up from his muddy spot in the shade of a big tree. When Bob opened the door, the boar caught wind of the milk and tore across the pen, grunting all the way. The sow jerked awake, lurching onto her legs, and followed. Stub poured one pail into the trough, and the boar was into it right away, pausing only to look up at them, as if in thanks, curds of soured milk clinging to his whiskers, before thrusting his snout back into it, gulping nonstop. The sow shouldered her way into position as Bob poured the second pail in; the boar nipped at her ear to reserve the first, largest wave of swill for himself.

"Apley appears to be burnt out," Stub said.

"Oh yeah?" Bob said. "What if he is?"

Stub watched the hogs going at it, grunting, gulping, looking up, and smacking their jaws. "So what."

"So what? Isn't your old man the guy who was supposed to be screwed? If Apley sells this place for condos he could make a fortune. And what did your dad get?"

Stub waved the hand with a missing finger at Bob. "He probably didn't get what he should of. But he agreed to it. The problem is, he's no longer a player. He can't come back like a ballplayer and renegotiate. It's over. Done."

"Yeah, but don't you wish you had this place to farm?"

"Who in his right mind farms today? That's like shooting heroin. It feels good for a while, but sooner or later you die. And you don't get half as much out of it along the way."

"I don't know about that," Bob said. "My brother would give anything not to have to work on the third floor of the factory where my father works. He comes home at night, his nose clogged with the brown dust of the particle board they use as insulator beneath electric switches. And I smell like cow dung but have nothing else up my nose except pollen."

"Good for you," Stub said. "But you don't own the place. You're just a visitor. A paid spectator. Owning it is a whole other trip."

"It's got to be worth it. At least you'd be better than some Waspy hog who owns a factory he wouldn't dare set foot in."

"And you're so swell," Stub said, and laughed. "You're an All-American boy. My brother would love you. But I don't give a shit. About farming. About what my father wails about. Apley may be a favorite on your side of the family, but I'm sick of hearing about him over here. About all the good cousins he's given jobs to. About all the good things he's done in town. It's all bullshit. What does he have to show for it? A son gone up north. A daughter-in-law who's a vegetable. A wife run off. No herd and no heirs. He's done a real good job, Apley has."

There was a pause, as if the conversation had reached a cliff. The sound of muffled, distant laughter filled the gap. Bob saw Abbott's trucks, parked farther up the road in the thicket. They had pulled in there to drink and play cards.

"Times are good for Abbott," Stub said. "Gets twenty bucks an hour knocking zinc nails in trees as the only way to stop the Dutch elm disease. When that fails, and it always does, he gets to saw them down and sell the firewood. He's got you coming and going. What a racket."

Down the road in the opposite direction, Bob saw Apley's truck pull into the farm. "Let's get the pails back," he said.

"And after that? We going swimming?"

"Yeah, up to Mohawk."

Stub pulled a joint from his pocket. "That's the spirit. To hell with farming."

•   •   •

By mid-August Bob still had a quarter of the roof left to shingle. The heat had been overwhelming. He had to get off the roof by eleven each morning. No rain—every day the same. The weatherman reported that it had rained several times, but that the drops evaporated before they hit the ground. At Mohawk Pond, the water had gotten warm and murky; its level was down a foot. Snakes slithered across the surface. You could see the rock ledge beneath the water. They had been the only ones there for two weeks. Stub still swung out upside down on the rope and dropped into the water, yelling "shiiit" as he fell. Bob couldn't bring himself to try it, stoned or straight.

The haze and heat surrounded Bob like a blanket. Nothing mattered anymore. He was secure. And better than that, he was pleased with the prospect of leaving everything he had ever known—home, menial work. It was all changing. Changing faster than he could have anticipated. After Apley left for business in town each day around ten, Bob took an ice tea break for an hour and read books, confident that he had found the first thing ever in his life he would call a break—a sudden departure from the routine of labor and fatigue he had known since childhood. Soon it would be Labor Day and time to head off to college. He would be caught up in the things he had always wanted to read about. He also had the luxury of knowing he didn't have to do the double shift in the college dining room that the financial aid guy had set up.

• • •

Bob was at the crest of the roof, hammering a few shingles, the sound echoing off the old chicken house and fading into the woods. From where he sat he could see the
alfalfa field, the brown patches spreading daily. There
would be no second cutting there. And Apley had sold
the hogs off the week before. Even the milking equipment
and coolers were gone; the barn was the only work left.
Bob could count the rows of shingles left to do. Maybe
one-fifth of the roof. Bob figured he needed five hundred
dollars more—maybe three more weeks—to eliminate
finding any job over and above his work-study. It would be
easy to drag the job out. Especially if Apley kept paying
him to take swims in the afternoon. Just before lunch,
Apley called him down from the roof. Then, at the kitchen
table, Apley told him he couldn't work anymore. Bob was
dumbstruck. All his scheming had been stripped away.
"I've sold the farm," Apley said calmly. "Hated to. But
it's done." Apley popped open a beer. "Join me?"
Bob shook his head. "Why shouldn't I finish the roof?"
"No insurance. I canceled it right after we signed the
papers yesterday." He winked at Bob. "No sense in paying
liability on something you don't own, right?"
"So you're just pulling out? Like that? No warning? I
could have found something else for three more weeks with
just a little warning. Now it will be almost impossible."
"I considered telling you along the way," he said, "but
held back. I didn't expect it to happen so fast. It doesn't
happen this fast very often. But the day after I put the place
on the market, my real estate man, Harold, he finds a
woman from Westchester County. Wanted another horse
farm."

"Who knows?"

"You're the first in the family. I suppose Harold's talking now." Apley took another beer from the refrigerator and popped it open, spraying Bob. "Not exactly champagne, but it'll do. Sure you won't join me?"

Bob shook his head. He felt like he had let a good thing slip through his hands. If he had been smarter, he would have negotiated a guaranteed amount of money for the summer.

Apley closed his eyes and leaned back in his chair. He sipped from his beer without setting the can down. He was tired. Bob could see that plainly. But there was something else. He seemed smaller and older than Bob had ever seen him. Bob realized Apley wasn't even as tall as he was. It had been that way for months, now that Bob thought about it. But he had held on to his first image of Apley: tall, strong, and lively. All of that had gone.

After Apley dozed off Bob went outside. He thought about calling his father for a ride home but decided to hitch into town. Stub's car pulled over just as he reached the main road.

"Climb in," Stub said.

Stub wasn't surprised by the news. Why would Apley keep farming, he asked. And if some rich horsewoman was going to give him more than the place was worth, why not sell it?

"How would you like to meet Ronnie?" Stub asked. "He's back home now that the day camp is shut down and his American Legion team isn't going to the tournament."

"I really just want to go home."

"C'mon," Stub said calmly. "Ronnie wants to smoke

with us. You shouldn't pass it up."

"Ronnie?"

"Big changes. Some kids at camp turned him on. He claims it improves the control of his curveball. Says he smoked before every game."

They turned onto the side road where Stub lived. The road wound up a gradual slope. The fields to the side were rockier than Apley's. If this was the land Apley had given his brother, Bob saw why there could be bad feelings. Stub's house was right next to the road, and smaller than the house Apley used for his barn hand. There was a two-stall equipment shed empty on one side, the other filled with a pickup on blocks. Farther off, a small barn that hadn't been painted in years. The crest of the roof bowed down at the center like the back of an old horse at the county fair.

Stub parked the Rambler next to an empty ceramic block silo without any roof. When Bob got out of the car, he realized he was standing on the foundation of a barn.

"What happened to the barn?" Bob asked.

"Burned ten years ago. The mastermind here was rewiring it." Stub motioned with his head toward the house. A man was walking toward them, holding the plastic netting of a six pack with one last beer dangling from it. His belly was swollen to the size of a basketball, and his face glowed red as if he had been facing a winter wind. Puffing, he tossed the plastic aside and opened the beer, taking a long swallow. He wiped his mouth with the back of his hand.

"You're Bob, I suppose. Ellie's boy."

Bob nodded. He started to offer his hand, but Andy raised the beer in a salute instead.

"Saw you once when you were at Tip Top's buying sneakers. You were going to start kindergarten."

"I'm sure he remembers, Andy," Stub said.

"So that's that," he said finally, puffing still. He kicked a pebble into the weeds.

"What?"

"Apley sold the place out from under all of us."

"Some lady with horses," Bob said.

"Sure. Just what the town needs. Another one of them. I'll bet he got her good for it, too. Huh?"

Stub nudged Bob. "Some other time, Andy. Tell him the whole story."

"He's a nutmegger, that bastard. And it says at the town hall he's my brother."

A tall, wiry boy stood on the porch. Bob guessed it was Ronnie. Bob wondered what Stub would look like with his brother's short hair.

"Maybe I'll get a lawyer and see if I can go after the son of a bitch," Andy continued. "Yeah, I like that idea."

"Hey, Ronnie, you coming with us, or not?"

"Pop," Ronnie said. "I'm going for a ride."

"Okay, champ," Andy said. "Hey, wait a second. Aren't you pitching in that pickup game tonight?"

"Tomorrow, Pop. That's tomorrow."

Andy nodded as if he had suddenly remembered. "Yeah, that's right," he said. "You boys take it easy."

"We take it any way we get it," Ronnie said, his breath smelling of peanut butter.

"Ha," Andy said. "That's the spirit."

Ronnie motioned Bob to the back seat. "No leg room for me back there. Do you mind?"

When they got to the main road, Ronnie rolled up his
window. "So, what's so hot about this shit you've got?" he
said to Stub.

"It's good," Stub said. "Very special."

"Special for what?" Ronnie asked.

"For shutting down the central nervous system," Stub
said.

"Oh, that," Ronnie said, looking confused.

Bob snickered in spite of himself. So this was the big
jock. He watched as Stub handed a joint to Ronnie. Stub
pushed the cigarette lighter in. When it popped out, Ronnie lit the joint, took a drag, and passed it to Stub.

"So, do you have a dog?" Ronnie asked Bob.

Bob nodded. "A Lab," he said.

"And have you been fucked today?" he asked.

Bob squinted at Ronnie. "Not as yet."

"You mean to tell me, you have a dog with an asshole and
you haven't been fucked today?" Ronnie lit up with laughter, buckling over in the front seat.

Bob glanced in the rearview mirror and saw Stub staring
at him, rolling his eyes.

"I'm hungry," Ronnie said.

"We have another joint," Stub replied.

"I'm hungry now," Ronnie said.

Ronnie ate three Whoppers at Burger King.

"You're going to have to watch your weight," Stub said.
"At least if you intend to smoke seriously."

"Yeah," Ronnie said. "Is it time to head home?"

"It's never time for that," Stub said.

"C'mon, I've got a date tonight," Ronnie said.

"We've only been gone an hour and a half," Bob said.

"Is that all?" Ronnie said. "Jeez, this shit is good."

"Just an hour and a half," Bob said.

Ronnie laughed and almost choked on a mouthful of french fries.

"Let's go," Stub said, suddenly seeming like he hadn't smoked at all. He drove them out of town, on a dirt road that ran alongside Pitch Reservoir. He stopped the car and they rolled down the windows. You could hear the wind in the pine trees, see a fish jump, smell the moist air. Then he started driving again. After a while, he pulled another joint from his pocket. He parked near the top of the dam. "Roll up the windows," he said. "This one is specially treated," he said.

Ronnie lit it up and took several long pulls. "I can take this," he said. "What's so special about this? You wimps got a problem with some man's shit?"

"It's opiated," Stub said.

Bob took a toke. He felt it immediately.

"So how is everyone?" Stub asked, sounding like a host.

"I'm good," Ronnie said, slowly.

"Are you sure?" Stub asked.

"Let me think," Ronnie said.

"You work on that while I ask Bob," Stub said. He turned to Bob. "And how's our guest on this family picnic?"

Bob thought he winked back, but it might have been a twitch. "I'm still here." They were driving again, the woods passing by slowly, and then they were on the main road. Bob had never before noticed how many houses had bird baths. "Why are the birds so dirty?" he asked.

Ronnie laughed. "Should I open the window?" he asked.

Bob didn't understand what that had to do with dirty birds.

"You don't need to ask permission," Stub said. "Open it whenever you like."

"Okay," Ronnie said. "I'm opening it now."

"Don't fall out," Stub said, and everyone laughed. "Maybe I should take you over to Coach Willink's house now."

"Oh, don't do that," Ronnie said.

"What would be wrong with that," Stub said as he turned onto a side road. "Doesn't he live somewhere up here?"

"Don't, Gene. C'mon."

As they neared a house with a brand-new Bronco parked next to the front door, Ronnie sank in the seat. Stub beeped the horn and slowed the car. "How about it?" he said.

"Don't do that," Ronnie pleaded.

Stub was speeding up again. Bob thought he saw someone looking out a window, but it might have been a reflection. Ronnie rose again and exhaled. "Thanks," he said.

"How about some donuts?" Stub asked.

Stub stopped at a Donut World and went inside.

"What's taking him?" Ronnie asked.

"It hasn't been that long," Bob said. Suddenly he remembered that the farm had been sold and wanted to go home.

Stub returned with two dozen jelly-filled donuts.

"I don't like these," Ronnie said, his mouth full.

"We're not going to eat them," Stub said. "We're going to throw them." Stub eased the car back onto the road.

"At what?" Ronnie asked.

"At signs. Can you hit a speed sign, Ron?"

Ronnie snorted. "Of course." At the sight of the first one, Ronnie leaned out of the window and tossed a jelly donut at a curve-in-the-road sign, hitting it dead center.

"Too easy," Bob said.

"You couldn't do it," Ronnie said.

"I'm not claiming I can. I meant it was too easy for you."

"Name something you think is harder."

"How about a mailbox?" Stub said.

"No problem," Ronnie said.

Stub increased the speed of the car as they neared the first mailbox. Ronnie threw the donut and missed.

"Ha," Bob said.

"Hey, slow down," Ronnie said, grabbing another donut. He leaned farther out of the car. He cocked his arm as they neared the next mailbox, and leaned still farther out. Bob grabbed the back of his jeans as he threw. Ronnie's hand slapped Bob's away.

"Keep your hands out of my pants, fag. You made me miss."

"I didn't want you to fall."

"Don't worry about it."

"I don't know," Stub said. "Two mailboxes, two misses. Good thing the scouts aren't watching."

"Just warming up. Give me one more chance. One more."

They were near Apley's when they spotted the next mailbox. "Slow down," Ronnie said.

"That makes it too easy," Stub said.

"Then I need a better angle," Ronnie said, thrusting his

entire upper body through the window. His knees were on
the seat. Bob grabbed him by the belt as he cocked his arm,
the car swerving toward the mailbox. It hung from chains
that had been welded stiff.

"Steady," Ronnie said. Bob tightened his grip on Ronnie's belt. The car jagged right. Bob heard a splat.

"He got it," Bob said.

"He sure did," Stub said.

"Get in," Bob said, pulling at Ronnie.

Ronnie shook as if he were cold. There was a funny
whine—Bob thought it was the wind. But as Ronnie slid
into the car, Bob realized where it was coming from. His
face was white, and he held his hand still in front of him.
Blood was all over it.

"He's hurt," Bob said.

Stub glanced at him. "A scrape. Shake it off."

Bob forced himself to look at it. His index and middle
fingers were bent over backward, dangling. Blood was spitting out over the seat.

"Get your hand out the window," Stub was saying.

Ronnie started rocking back and forth. There was another sound. A high-pitched noise, growing louder. It was
Ronnie. He was wailing now. One long wail.

Stub made a U-turn in front of another car and acceler-
ated rapidly. He ran a red light at the center of town. The
trip took forever, Ronnie wailing loudly, then softly as if
he were resting, and then loudly again. As they reached the
hospital, it started to rain big, oversized drops, soaking
straight through their shirts as they took Ronnie into the
emergency room. There was the smell that hot asphalt
gives off as it rains.

Later, after Andy had come and they had heard that no fingers were lost and that, in the opinion of the doctor, Ronnie was a lucky young man and would probably regain as much as fifty percent of their use, Stub and Bob walked back to the car.

"You swerved on purpose," Bob said.

Stub stopped in the rain and grinned at Bob. "The jerk had his hand out too long, that's all. He's lucky he didn't leave it on the chain."

On spring break from college Bob saw Ronnie in town. His father had died. His liver gave out, Ronnie said. Bob asked how Ronnie's hand was.

"My pitching days are over," Ronnie said. "The school couldn't see its way clear to keep me on. So I'm back at the place. Trying to raise Shetlands."

Bob glanced at the hand. "I'm sorry," he said, immediately realizing that was the last thing he should say.

"Don't be," Ronnie said. "Heck, it still does the basics: holds a beer and gets down a girl's pants."

"You heard from Stub?" Bob asked.

Ronnie shook his head. "He's gone. We didn't even know how to get hold of him for the funeral. Have you?"

Bob lied and shook his head. At Christmas there had been a postcard waiting for him at home. The photo side showed Thomas Edison. His parents said they hadn't read it, but Bob didn't believe them. It was postmarked from Schenectady. Stub wrote that he was working in an RCA distribution warehouse. "I take one or two TVs a week—everyone

does. We call it damaged merchandise. They pay for groceries. I might not be back."

"Did Apley make the funeral?" Bob asked.

"Oh, yeah. He and his new lady friend."

"And who's that?"

"The horsewoman who bought the place."

"I heard he was just a consultant to her."

"Ha," Ronnie said. "That's a good one. He's officially the
manager of the place. His deal is sweeter than that. I guess
you could say he's back in the saddle again." With that,
Ronnie slapped Bob on the back with his crippled hand.
"That's the one thing I miss about college. All the girls. I
might take out a second mortgage on the place just to pay
for it. At least one more year of that life. But, hell, I don't
need to tell you."

Bob stuck out his lower lip and shook his head.

"Ha," Ronnie said. "You take it easy."

"I take it any way I can, Ron," Bob said, disgusted by the
sound of his own voice.

"Ha. That's the spirit."

Bob watched Ronnie drive off. The first semester had
been tough for him. He had written more papers in three
months than he had in four years of high school. He hadn't
done well. Not as well as he was used to doing. When he
read the postcard, he envied Stub. He wanted TVs to steal,
too. Something that would pay for groceries. He wanted a
life other than the one he had so meticulously worked for.
A life like Apley's, where everything was lost only to come
out better in the end. Not a Horatio Alger novel. No, in the
book he liked to imagine as his life, a series of mean things

came about. Things that erased everything you had worked for. Only, at the end, just short of total destruction, you came out with money. And love. And with the sense that every bad break had been made worthwhile.